No. thirteen

By rj Longren

Did I know the other 12? Did I know their bodies were still in the house? It was always quiet and I could hear my breath, my heartbeat, his panting as he belted me. After a while I did not think of the sounds or the time draining away. I thought about the strength of the rope around my wrists and ankles. I waited. Most importantly I waited.

I'm not a pretty girl, or even a slim one. I wonder what the other girls looked like as he once told me how much he liked my dark brown eyes. He was a handful of inches taller than me. Blonde, The sight of him took my breath away. His eyes could be the coldest grey, then nearly blue. He had a strong rasp to his voice. He was always warm against my skin. He would press my shoulders down to the bare wood floor and draw up my crouch into his palm.

I was naked and cold. He stood over me in the dark. I waited listening then I felt his fingers on my lips. He leaned in and kissed me one last time because I will never get his taste out of my mouth. He shushed me and slid a threaded needle through my lips. He sewed them shut with three neat Xs. I didn't make a sound, not when the needle passed threw my upper lip and the little knot anchored inside. I couldn't twitch, I nearly passed out.

It was a warm night in early summer when I met him. I cried as the cold night air hit me when I left his house finally. I shot him right between his dull grey eyes and then I let myself out and began walking down the street. I was naked, missing my right eye and there was still blood fresh down my face. I remember the cop who pulled up and the face he made when he saw my sewn lips. It was the same face the EMT made as he snipped the threads.

It's hard to gauge time after so much of it passes unmarked without the sun on my face or even the chime of a clock. I'll attempt to tell you my tale from the beginning to end. How I met him, and fell in love with his touch. I should tell you about him and I will. He didn't close his eyes when I put the bullet between them.

I was reading the side panel to a cereal box when I caught my first glimpse of him. Clean-shaven, a ball cap and a clean well worn pair of jeans, he didn't stand out. Summer was teasing us; most of the other shoppers carried their jackets. He wore a t-shirt that draped his lean frame. I don't eat cereal often and really had no interest in purchasing the box I was reading but he slowly meandered down the aisle toward me. He took out a pack of gum and offered me a piece. I put the cereal back and as I took the gum from his hand, I got that first sweet whiff. We walked through the grocery. I'm not even sure why I was there. The hissing fluorescent lights baring us in white before we slipped into the night. I was transfixed.

I loved the dark sweet nights of my youth out at all hours trapping lightning bugs in jars. I would lay in the grass and open the lid letting the bugs fly over me. Their slow flash moving against the starry night.

Memory is a tricky thing. I know he must have driven me home with him. Some details became lost in the sound of his voice. If I close my eyes I can still smell him and hear him. he never told me his name and I never said mine either. In fact I spoke very little and then none at all. The living room was bare except for a black leather couch, a radio and long thin coffee table. He examined my hands and drew me closer to him after a few minutes. The couch was soft and had over the years become a part of his scent. I smelled the couch and I ran my nose along his chest inhaling until he pushed me down onto the couch. He put his thumb against my collar bone and spread his hand over my shoulder. He smiled. I smiled as he pulled off my pants and ripped my panties. I felt myself pant as his eyes became blue. After he finished undressing me he arranged me on the couch draping my hands over each other above my head. I gasped my lip quivered. He took me first facing him and then away. Then he threw me on the floor and began beating me with his belt across my thighs and ass. As quickly as he laid five or six strokes he paused his breath hard and he took his breath in sharply. I passed out there on the floor.

I woke up as the water hit my face. I could feel the warm water and the tub as I began to open my eyes. He bathed me and I laid my head on the side of the tub as he inspected my skin. Scrubbed every inch before rinsing me off and he ran his fingers through my hair. His nose twitched and he drew up his lip as his hand rounded the top of my head. He pushed my head in the water and I slide below the surface where I could still see his face. I closed my eyes letting my breath roll out. I heard the bubbles burst as he pulled me up by chin then putting both hands in the water he lifted me out of the tub. I laid on a plastic sheet which was covering the floor he left me there shutting the door behind him. I could see his shadow right outside the door. I thought about nothing letting myself pass out again.

I think about the plastic now sometimes. Was he going to kill me? Right then? In a few days? Months perhaps? The door opened and he stepped back in swiftly bending over to gather me up leaving the plastic on the floor. He put my face in his chest as he carried me, once again I was on the couch. Naked and wet he wore only his jeans sitting down next to me. He watched me watch him and a smile came across his face slowly. He ran his hand over his zipper and laid it across his belly. As he leaned forward he grasped my ankles and dragged me into his lap hand over hand. Resting my thighs on his thighs I sat face to face on his lap and I smiled from ear to ear. He pushed my hands behind my back and cuffed them together. I throbbed basking in his warm lips on me. Then he turned me over and beat me moaning after the loud smacks.

I trembled on the floor as he rolled up a newspaper. I felt the pages leave slits in my skin. I heard the paper hit the floor , his footsteps as he left the room, the foot falls faded and rose. He snapped the belt then nuzzled my thigh with the bend before laying into my naked rear end. I know I lost consciousness. I know I slept.

The cop went in the house leaving me with the EMT, the door was standing open and he returned calling loudly for back up "I've got a body in a bedroom and 12 more in a walk in freezer. At ….." I began to think about the other girls.

His living room opened into a kitchen, down a little hallway were three doors. The first door was the bathroom with stark white tile under an old claw foot tub. I remember laying in the tub resting my head against the folded lip. The window over the tub was small and heavily frosted small specks of light would dance on the closed door. This door faced the front and was only a few feet from the second which was never open. At the end of the hallway on the same side as the bathroom stood the third and it was only closed when I was inside. The floor was wood running from the living room through the hallway and down to the third room.

The house was dark and quiet. Even the floor boards shushed as his feet sled over them. I lay in the tub listening to my own heartbeat. There was no light under the door. I heard the handle turn as he stepped inside towel draped over his bare shoulder. His pale chest was also bare shutting the door behind him he laid the towel on the floor and kneeled down beside the tub. The downy hairs of his body looked as soft as the remaining crown of hair left on the back of his head. The water was still warm and he cupped his hand to dampen my hair and shoulders. My eyes were fixed on

9

him. My lips parted slightly as I sighed. He stroked my lower lip and pinched it then slipped his finger over the top lip pinching them closed. This still left his left hand on my shoulder as I watched his eyes run down my body as they began to become clear blue. My heart quickened as I anticipated his hand's path between my legs. He thrust two fingers inside me watching my face. I opened my legs relaxing my body letting every fiber become liquid. I felt a need to give into his desire, to give into his touch. I kept my eyes open watching his face. He let out a sigh and pulled his hand up my hip and then my rib cage. Running his thumb along my nipples which he gazed at before leaning forward and then using both hands to sit me up in the tub. My chest ached and I felt a pain in my hip as I rested my weight upon it. I closed my eyes. Nicotine layered with his musky scent, the bathroom itself was absent, nil to my nose. Bruises down my thighs, purple and blue as he pulled the plug letting the water out.

I passed out as the EMT snipped the threads from my lips. I heard the sirens as faint echoes. I slept unable to open my eyes and unable to produce words. I smelled the ointment feeling the nurse paint my lips, my cheek tight where the tape stuck holding a thick pad of cotton over my right eye. Looking up into the ceiling I heard the nurse greet me. She smiled "you're safe now, and we even were able to give you a new right eye." I turned my head trying to survey the room but found that I was too stiff to move. Vomit rushed up my dry throat as I nearly fell out of the bed trying to not choke on it.

His towels were fluffy white barely used and he would dry me off as I kneeled on the bathroom floor. I felt a pick in my backside and a warm metal taste rise in my lips. Down the hall he carried me to the third room shutting the door behind us. On my side I faced the door as he bound my wrists together and then to the bed leg. He lay there his hand stroking my shoulder as I fell into unconsciousness.

I heard the snap of the doctor's clipboard opening my eyes, the right one blocked with cotton. Then his voice as he told two men that I would have full use of both my eyes soon. I turned my head toward the side the doctor was facing seeing both men in suits standing beside the railing. They fussed over me removing the pad from my right the doctor then filled my eye with drops until the liquid ran down my face. I blinked hard focusing on his face. The men introduced themselves as detectives on the homicide unit producing badges and one a notebook. They read me my rights stating that I would not be formally charged until enough information was obtained. Then they asked me if I could answer some questions. My lips felt heavy I took a deep breath pushing my lungs against my tender ribs and found nothing to say. Tears rolled down both sides of my face. The doctor called in a nurse as I fought for breath. As I felt every word die in my mouth. I saw her pop the needle into the last section of IV the nurse watched my heart beat smooth out as she injected me. I heard her heels over the doctor's thinning voice he said my heart is broken.

The sheets were pale blue, the blanket a thermal cotton white. My hands were bound together by the wrists the rope snaked over the edge down the floor. I was sore and felt the weight of his body pinning me as he pulled the sheet and blanket down to my ankles. Face down he squeezed my butt in a fat pinch I felt the needle melt into my skin. My rubbery limbs slipped up behind me as he re tied my arms. He gathered my wrists one stroke as the rope slopped across my lower back. The cup of his hand pushed each knee into the bed and then under my navel drawing my ass up. He gagged me shoving his cock into my mouth cradling my head as the belt sailed down across my thighs. He straddled my face and the belt became louder and faster. I felt the floor before I heard my body embrace it. The belt still drumming my flesh he flipped me up to my knees his hand across my throat his breath was heavy on my face. His blue eyes engorged by each pupil. Then I whimpered softly. He leaned in and sunk his teeth into my throat bending me backward in his arms until my arms hit the floor and on my side he slipped the belt around my neck. His hot lips on my ear shush he said shush. As the belt tightened I couldn't fight, my pounds become ounces. The sweat droplets sizzled on my skin. I oozed him. I slipped away into the air. I let the life escape my misery. I went and came until I drew a hard nasty breath. The buckle plopped on the floor as if I had coughed it up. He tossed me up on the bed rolling me almost over the other side before jerking me into the middle. Face down he mounted me and wordlessly he took me stopping only to beat me. I quivered my bones jelly as I tried to hold myself up. I could hear the force of his breath sucking the room walls in and pushing me out through his lungs. He moaned twitching his hip and spilled out my throbbing flesh I felt a hot rush and he took the belt, buckle at the end, to my mound in long hard flaps. I cried out. One hard vowel stopped the air. Off the bed into the wall my shoulders flipped me onto the floor. He flipped me over fingers over my lips. Shush he put a finger to his lips. Shush.

Is this how it all starts? That one suggestion of guilt. The seed of an ill thought that becomes every breath of the day and night. I find myself courting a death wish. Is it death that smells so sweet or his musky skin? Is it my will to live or an inability to die that drives my heart to keep my veins flowing. I am filled with guilt as my desire betrays me. I want to give in. I want to leave every bit of flesh behind.

The hiss of air becomes the first note in the sound of my conscious. The dull beep pulls out a long scratch. My lips thick under my fingers I slowly caress my face closing my left to look through my new right eye. A uniformed officer sleeps propped up on his elbow on the arm of a chair. His radio hesitantly prickling the sound of my breath. I finger the silver rail testing its surface, testing my grip. I pull my weight to rest on my elbow and I can see the night outside the window. It's concrete and chirping without wind. I feel warm as if cradled in a soft silken gown. Sitting up I push the blanket down my legs. I count my toes wiggling them. I let out a thin slow breath crying helplessly. As quickly as the tears run down I run dry. The man snores startling me. I watch the sun fill the window the room glows in the morning light. I squint in the thrown open door which wakes the cop who falls forward. One of the suited detectives accompanies the doctor. He has coal black hair ,a permanent five o'clock shadow and taps his notebook across his palm. A nurse brings in a tray setting it on the stand before draping me over the side of the bed. I stand finding the tile floor under my bare feet.

"can you tell me your name? perhaps your birthday? Where you were born?" I took a breath hoping the answers would be in the air in my lungs. "would you like to write it down?" the doctor had a yellow legal paid and a plain black pen. He scooted the little tray up to my side and laid the pen across the paper facing me. My hands ached. I gripped the pen and carved my name into the top line. I wrote No. thirteen.

The detective introduces himself Det. Nervous with the notebook drumming his palm. "Can you answer a few questions?" Nervous flips backward in his notebook. I wrote No. thirteen. "She's in no condition for questioning she clearly is in shock." The doctors shuffle the cops out leaving me with a trail of doctors.

I shook the psychologists hands. I started to wonder how many doctors were doing rounds in this building. I kept hearing the word Stockholm and shock traded between the suits and white coats. The words permeated my skin as I lay in the warm sheets.

My eyes can see the rope tied around my wrists as breath fills my cold lungs, I am the warmth in the blue sheets. All alone with my thoughts I begin to long for his moist lips and even the wet belt whips. Silence stalks the stillness, I can not bear it but I can not push anything but air out. Gingerly I pull my wrists towards me an unsteady act only when the rope draws across the bed taunt, in a hard tug it gives way jarring my shoulder. I cup my hands fingers inching the rope through them. Its silver and glows faintly against the pale cotton sheet. The door opens letting in light and him. he stands there his shadow over my hands. For a moment I hold my breath as he steps to the side of the bed. Another hard pinch and I slack letting the fingers of one hand droop. He unties one of my hands to spread my arms out post to post on the bed, secures each hand to separate ends. Over me he slips his fingers down each arm tugging them to check his knots. With a hot breath he turns my face one side and then the other peering into the eye. I feel the slippery warmth rippling my veins. Then the rope around each ankle first the right snaking the rope taunt pulling my back flat. The left wound and his teeth sink into my toes before he licks between them. I want to know what will become of me but I'm already sure that I won't feel any of it.

Most people have a love affair with death. They use other words and names but there is only so many ways one can dress up such desires. Adrenaline junkies claim that their acts of reckless endangerment give them a lust for life but most people are grateful to be alive. Death is destructive and powerful striking us clean of time, knowledge and every ounce of consciousness. If the human condition is to suffer then death is the only cure. In this mortal world after decades of self discovery we have learned that eliminating threats prolongs but a life without strife and struggle becomes the very thing we are escaping. I tell you that I am far too honest. Possibly one of few women unable to lie with my loins. It's not a fatal flaw because it's not the only one and it's not a flaw unless it ruins something. Since I was always ruined, my flaws are the things that hold me together. I have no fear of death. I've long ago allowed myself to realize I have no control over death or life. People want to believe their lives happen for a reason. What if life is it's own purpose? What if it's less reason and more chance? I can see how most do their best to be responsible for their involvement. I'm not a fan of group belief. All I can profess to know is what I have taken in. There are times I'm not sure any of it is not a figment of my own consciousness.

The smell of the wood floor wet with my odor as I tremble on my knees, hands tied behind me and his legs straddling me. The flat of his palm slaps and squeezes before he slips me down further to the floor. Spread out to the wood he covers me with his body wrapping a hand across my throat and tells me how he loves me and the others weren't meant for him. all mine he says this is all mine. The hard thumb in my throat moves up my jaw line and two of his fingers go in my mouth. I feel my breath come hard with his breath. Everything slows down we breath the soupy air as if we shared a near collapsed lung.

I can hear the tapping of Det. Nervous. His pen lighter than the notebook, he scratches before sighing, taps his foot impatient for his answers. His drugstore cologne doesn't cover the cigarette smell. He might drink coffee or pop those caffeine tablets trying to stay sharp through out his shift, but it only seems to have caught him jitters. He mutters to himself then addresses me. " 13 women and 12 wrapped in plastic, thirteen the only one alive, the only one missing an eye, the only one to survive longer than three days. … "

I think of him now as I lay here in the hiss of the machines interrupting my dreams. Heavy curtains keep out the stark Arizona sun but the pale unnatural fluorescent light seeps through out the room neatly illuminating all the square inches of white floor and white walls. His pale skin as his hands traced the thin bruises along my arms where the ropes tightened. I could feel the weight of his body against me as I slept tethered to the bed always by my wrists. There wasn't an inch of me that didn't accommodate him. the hard throb of his heart set the pace of my own. His voice was the sound, his fury crushed and ebbed inside my flesh. It was not his pleasure I came to share but the longing to escape. Alone with my thoughts and the constant beeping, I have always treasured silence when ever it came upon me. Rarely is the world dampened, the light of day exposing the cracks in the cement of civilization. In his house the halted world bore no pull on me. My conscious was unable to grasp time, the concept of a day or even a night slipped through my breath. He sat on the edge of the bed, plate in his lap and fed me. My bound wrists often over my head or behind my back. He ate with me sharing meatloaf or fried chicken with mashed potatoes and corn. In the bathroom there were needles and vials after being bathed he would secure me in bed and with the prepared syringe inject my shoulder with morphine. The sweet metallic taste would fill my mouth, I would look forward to each nip as it swept me away.

The Doctor gives me morphine but the doses are smaller. I sit up in the hospital bed propped up with pillows. I wonder about Det. Nervous where he might be and what he knows. All the nurses draw my blood, turning the TV on to shield themselves from silence. As soon as they leave I turn it off allowing my thoughts to run off with me. The absence of smell sharpens my need to remember his scent but it is no longer on me. I don't want to speak worried about secrets that spill out will end my warm memories. There must be forgotten moments, brutal and cruel desire in both our hearts. My dormant yearning to destroy every life including my own. Each of my ribs ache, the patch has been removed from my right eye. I toss back the blankets my legs pale and blue have started to twitch. I swing them over the side and stand holding the bed rail. Tugging on my IV I locate which rolling rack it's attached to and pull it with me backwards to separate it. Almost forgetting the heart monitor before making it to the end of the bed. The sensor pops off snapping my arm setting an alarm off. I run my hands over the sides flipping the power switch silencing it. I listen for footfalls down what must be the hallway behind the closed door. After I am convinced no one is rushing towards me I use the IV pole to shuffle into the well lit musky bathroom. In the mirror over the sink I face my one blue eye. I am thin, gaunt and my brown hair runs in a shock down my neck. Removing the thin gown I look my skin over. I feel delicate, hollow standing beside the IV pole my left hand twisted around it. My right hand flat on the upper lip of the sink as I lean in to focus my new eye. It's blue nearly white as it catches a reflection of the bar of light over the mirror. My breath fogs the mirror as I hear the outer door open and see Det. Nervous step into the frame of the bathroom door. He turns around and holding open the door calls for the nurse who pushes Det. Nervous back into the hallway. She steps into the bathroom and closes the door. I can hear the Doctor outside telling Nervous that this harassment will not be tolerated. "this woman is very ill, and it is paramount that she not be stressed." "of course she's stressed she shot a man between the eyes. Look Doctor she is the only thing alive from a house with 12 dead frozen girls and 1 bullet in the man's head. I need her statement." "for the time being thirteen is in my medical and the government's legal care. You will have to get your paperwork in order because I will not tolerate this interruption of her rest." I can hear the Detective whispering before his heavy footfalls recede. I'm still standing in the bathroom with the nurse tying my gown when the Doctor knocks on the door. "Are we decent in there?" the nurse opens the door and helps me back to the bed. She washes my feet and dries them as the Doctor flips through a file in his hand. Soft socks slide up to my knees the Doctor smiles as the nurses tucks me in. They leave the room together after a few minutes the nurse returns with two cups one small and plastic filled with baby blue and white caplets the other a paper cup with water. The water is not cold but the pills are and I watch her waiting for me to swallow. She leaves me alone again turning the TV on and as soon as the door claps closed I silence it. I begin to fidget and this silence becomes unaired. I shift in the bed listening to the sheets rustle I lift one hip and then the other then pause. I try to hold my breath but my lips pucker out gasping for air. I can hear myself the loud throb of my heart and the hot tears pouring down my face. My open mouth biting the air hissing and then dropping my lips together I turn them upward tightly closing my eyes. Ready to take my last breath as long as my lungs can pull. But I flinch losing myself in the interrupting noise. My tongue feels swollen and there is not a word ready to use. There is not one word worth speaking first than any other. But all of them turn to silence mashed in my brain together. I'm unsure of how my voice sounds I remember his fingers over my lips "Mm" I was saying and shush he was saying. I remember how his fingers tasted, I smile pulling my lips slightly over my teeth. I would rest my teeth on his fingers as he put them in my mouth. Once I bit down, he flipped me over and putting my lips together in his fingers he shushed me before he slapped me in the face. I cried while he forced open my legs. He slapped me again and I cried quietly staring at him while he finished. He met my eye closing his eyes only as he came before taking the belt to my naked body. He said nothing and I passed out quickly as he licked the hot wet tears from my face.

The tapping of the notebook wakes me but it's the pen light that makes me open my eyes. My right has become crusty and the Doctor clears it with a wet wipe his lips closed as he peers into my blue eye then cupping my jaw he turns my face. Det. Nervous stands at the foot of the bed his five o'clock shadow overtaking his face with thick black fur. Shifting his weight he flips it open reading a few pages his lips open mumbling. Through the door two men in suits follow a white coated white haired doctor. The room turns as he scoops up the file and clearing his throat turns to me, his eyes meeting mine before smiling . "such a popular girl" he peers over the open file before sitting on the end of the bed. "we all want to help you" I sit up rolling forward and leaning on the tray. Det. Nervous taps faster leaning in. there's not a note in me. I lick my lips. I sigh letting the air out slowly. The double white doctor takes out a pen from his shirt pocket "No. thirteen is aware of herself now but only in reference to recent history. If someone had used her name that might have registered but since the information has all been kept from her she is still a prisoner." Det. Nervous taps his notebook five times. "I haven't ruled out murder for my male victim"

"it had to be murder because her life was dependent on it." "I'm not convinced that No. thirteen felt she was in danger of losing her life." Det. Nervous refers to his notebook. "there are enough deviations from the other twelve women to led any jury to believe No. thirteen might be …"

"Look detective the 12 counts of murder against your male victim and the breath still in No. thirteen an intended victim is going to make you charging her silly. As her doctor I will not sign off on this harassment you will not be dropping in to check on her progress. I will call you, someone will be in touch. " as Det. Nervous strides out of the room digging in his coat.

He told me how he loved me as he untied me and slipped me into bed. He sat in a plain wooden chair, stroking my hair and humming. I think about the way his hands drifted over my body. He would lick his lips and then his teeth before kissing my bare back leaning over me. Getting into the bed he would lay on me and wrap his hands around my wrists. The even sound of his breathing would soothe me.

The double white doctor snaps his fingers as I gasp drowning in my sedated drool I wipe my mouth using the back of my left hand. Two orderlies tug me into a sitting position they are large men one of them is quite tall but thin and reedy. He hesitates to place my right hand in my lap I eyeball him feeling like a doll being draped. His eyes meet mine as he holds his breath stepping back before setting my hand on my thigh. Double white clears his throat "you are safe. No harm will come to you here. I want to reassure you that everything you tell me will be confidential. There is no reason to fear the thoughts in your head, share them with me. tell me about before your lips were closed. But I don't think it started there and we need to find where it started. Help me help you."

He snaps closed the file and rising watching me he turns to the orderlies who escort him out closing the door leaving me alone. I can hear the birds but even at night one can hear birds in the summer. It felt like a long summer. I spent it in his arms pressed between sheets preserved. I woke up face to face with him a dusty ray across his ear. There was a little scar on his face I ran my finger over it as he opened his eyes. He opened his mouth and took a couple of my fingers into his mouth. I felt my eyes well up as he stared me down. Kissing my face he licked the tears I couldn't stop and pushing me out of bed I landed on the floor under him. already naked he set me up on my knees face down on the wood. A fish rolling over on dry concrete I flipped arching my back he slapped me his left hand on my throat and right back hand not breaking his hold. Several times until my face was dry. He paused to return my face to the floor mounted me grunting he put his weight into me. I lost consciousness. But I still hear the birds.

In the day time the desert is a vacuous place where things slowly creep towards death. Where life is slowed by the stark sun melting the minutes into hours. I love the nights though when the moon drips it's honey glow across miles of dried out earth. It's dangerous a smell that not only whets my appetite but dampens my skin. Out in the desert night time ripples in the summer heat. I cross my morning to find that night, that moment I got off his floor and turned to walk out the door. I never touched the handle but I felt it's sweaty edge on my fingers like the sting of the belt buckle. I screamed the vowel swallowing the consonant. His foot on my chest as I lay on the floor my breath coming hard as I look up. The smile spreading my lips out as he smiles. There is a scratch down his chest he runs his finger over it and smudges my face with the blood. I roll grabbing his foot and bringing his weight down on me. I lick the scratch crouched over him. he rubs my face into his chest. We sat there on the floor in a heap listening to birds. Listening to the throb of our hearts trapped beneath our chests. I let out a deep sigh and stood up licking my lips my rib cage ached. "where are you going?" he tilted his head. A smile spread my lips as I let out my breath. I turned around and put my hand on the handle even stepped into the hallway. I stood in the hallway listening to his wide full breaths as he rested his hands on my hips. I walked into the living room bathed in midday sun it stunned me and I fell to my knees. I gasped and he dragged me back down the hallway grabbing my left hand and left foot.   The edge of the bed knocked the air from my lungs and he quickly tied each limb down testing the other limbs from each angle. He turned off the lights shutting the door. "I thought I was doing all the talking here? You need help shutting your mouth? I know what you need." I felt his fingers over my lips as he leaned in to kiss me. "mm" I was saying and shush he kissed me. The needle slipped into my lip like popping a balloon. It burst out the other side and the little knot stopped, my tongue could touch the end of the thread.   Then he tapped the needle tip against my lower lip three times before slipping it through both lips before tugging it tight. Again he tapped the needle tip closer to center but only twice before tightening the stitch. He completed the first X then slapped my face making me tighten the stitch. He laced his fingers under my chin and completed the second X pulling it tight with his teeth. Spitting on the needle as he rubbed it against where the third stitch would soon be, he told me he loved me. The he slowly slide the needle through my lips finishing the last X.   As he anchored the second knot he licked my threaded lips.

I slept in my hospital bed drawing my legs into my chest I don't feel safe here despite what double white says. I haven't seen Det. Nervous but I doubt his questions have been answered. I feel sad. I lay in the white cream glow of the hospital until the weight of my breath fills my eyes dripping those black thoughts out. He slipped my limbs from the tie downs holding me face to face while he licked my swollen lips. I drifted off in his arms.

I'm filled with barbarous words splitting my throat before my tongue can deliver them to my lips. I push my back upward thrusting myself into a kneel on the narrow firm hospital bed. I fling my head forward and crouch there on all fours looking at the door waiting unsure if there was anything to have been heard. The huff of my breath slows I feel it draw a hard but solid rhythm I am the only thing stirring in the night. I finger my lips feeling the little ruts left by thread. My hands are smooth smelling of my blood and sweat, I am overwhelmed and each tears slips down my cheek onto my hands down one finger I put the tear to my lips I pucker before pulling my lips over my teeth. " shush" I lick my finger closing my eyes and wiping my face with my hands I think about his lips and his tongue. I think about the way he made my leg shake until my heart would burst and every inch of my body would stop. I died in his arms, on his floor, under his hands millions of times. I look over at the heart monitor I'm attached to, my corded babysitter. The screen shows colored lines I lay back turned to it and then hand over hand draw the cord into the bed until I tugged the monitor bedside. The one time I turned it off it had been several minutes before any one came through the door. I thought about all my little deaths. I never closed my eyes even as my heart dropped out of chest and I felt my limbs slip away. Many times eye to eye he would not blink while I waited for my body to suck at the air. While I rested suspend inside my own flesh for the ripple of survival instinct to demand life, he was not patient and often the slap of his hand or the tear in his eye would fill my lungs and kick me alive. How could I leave him? Where could I go if I left here? The line throbs heaving itself across the monitor I watch it become steady. The thigh high socks feel heavy pressing into my thighs I roll them down to my knees angry red marks, stray thin red lines I can feel the scabs under my legs. Mm I find myself saying I slip my fingers up my thigh. I can almost smell the belt as the monitor's line flickers like a strobe. The buzzer sounds and I grope the air as it cuts off the line rolling confidently from side to side. I pull myself up the bed pulling the sheet over me before the door bursts open two nurses driving a cart stop eyes meeting mine before the second nurse turns driving the cart out the door. The first nurse busily checks the monitor sliding it back into the row next to the wall, she turns towards me inspecting the buttons stuck to my chest. Her weight resting on the bed she rearranges my bedding and I can tell she is waiting for double white to swing open the door sauntering in clipboard in the second nurse's hand signing it as he sighs. He faces me and the first nurse drags a chair out of the corner handing it to him before standing hands folded in front of her while he sits down. The second nurse has returned and hands him my green file. I know it's mine he brought it the last time but this time he spreads it out on the foot of the bed. Its reports and numbers, there is an outline of his house floor plan. The little red dots on the couch and the bed in the room where I slept, the floor and in the hallway and kitchen, but none in the garage or front bedroom. There are blue dots overlapping the red ones. double white clears his throat.

"you will be taking little walks around the grounds chaperoned or escorted however you wish to feel about it. You can go swimming, use the gym as well as attend group activities." He thrust the tip of his tongue through his cheek after which he gathered up the papers and piled them neatly into the green jacket. His pocket sings as he pushes the chair back into its corner. I don't recognize the tune. Not at first but it slipped into my head I could hear him singing, humming it. He began to take me from room to room I would sit in the kitchen watching him cook then eat. I hear the door shut as double white leaves the room.

There really is no such thing as complete silence. There is absences and muffed sometimes even leaked but never completely voided. He filled the sound in my world and took it away. lost me in a garbled word or slipped unsaid needs on me as he often covered my mouth after whispering his love in my ear. We never watched TV or listened to anything from the world beyond his walls. He would hum sometimes singing as he fused around the kitchen before cooking. I sat on a tall stool hands tied folded in my lap. Tied with a bow, I would cross my ankles as he kneeled tying the second bow then anchoring them to the stool. He would let me smell the food on his breath as he licked my face. He drank tea and there were different ones but mostly earl grey, warm with honey. The stainless steel pans were 12 inches and the first time he hit me I heard the singe before I felt it hit. Since my stool was wedged in a corner the walls cradled me as I slipped side to side one smack in a slow tennis game. He would tell me how he doubted my love for him and I would well up with tears. How I was some whore he picked up at the store and not good enough to be his. The first time, he untied me from the stool, he stood me at the edge of the kitchen and shouted at me that I was a whore he found at the store. He faced me towards the door and then paced in the kitchen behind me with heavy footfalls. I stood there resting my weight square on my hips as I stepped forward I turned listening to the absence of the floor, the warmth of his moist mouth caught me off guard and dropped me to the floor landing on me he sat up on my turned hip. I was naked and cold but every part of me was cold like a solid steel bar. The beat of my heart rippled my skin. Gathering me up in his arms he would tell me how he loved me whispering it in my ear my lucky girl. My lucky girl as he tapped my arm to pop more metal into these chilly veins.

A nurse is tapping my door sliding through it her cap pinned in her hair she chirps like a bird nothing she says sounds like words. I stare at her as she sits me up and dresses me putting a robe across my shoulders and drawstring pants as she lifts me to my feet. Standing she looks at me and then the heart monitor then presses the white button in my bed. The second nurse pops in with her clipboard and she tells Birdie to make sure to put down the actual time I go offline then asks if this floor can get a mobile one for me. Birdie chirps quite musically happy but what ever she said second nurse didn't like and scowled when she took her clipboard back. All my wires are laid out on the bed the little white circles carefully wiped off. Birdie chirps excitedly pausing to watch my face before going on with her song. As she finishes her song she has left all the drawers empty and arranged several plastic Ziploc bags on the bed. She takes a deep sigh as second nurse wheels in a wheel chair. I turn toward Birdie as she sings a few lines for second nurse and then taking my arm like the dance awaits I walk with her through the door into the hallway. It's short and yellow the elevator is waiting for us and Birdie sings as we step in two men in white scrubs take me up where Birdie hands off. We ride in silence up the elevator and I can smell the antiperspirant of each orderly and I turn my head right and then left hoping one of them wears his brand. The jolt of the elevator and both doors opening to Double white feels like being engulfed in fumes the minute the slit in the doors widened. I sneeze falling onto dark blue tile. Double white helps me up Birdie singing to him while taking files from his hands. He turns to the orderlies at my sides and I pull my arm back from the right one and then taking a step forward the left one drops my arm. They step back into the elevator Birdie staying with us I watch the doors swallow them as Double white and Birdie walk me down a much longer hallway. My thighs feel cold without the stockings, I examine the floor as we stop in a big open room. I follow the tile further with my eyes taking in the couches and chairs I see the TV then hear it's mumbling buzz. A woman stands leaning on the far wall her right hand poised as if holding a forgotten cigarette. I hear a plane but then see a woman carefully coaxing a book onto a table. The few men here are all in white, the women in thin pale blue robes like mine. Birdie wears all pink even her cap and the paint on her finger nails. Her song is barely audible the higher notes only reaching me. As she opens a white door off the hallway she turns towards me and waving into the room sings her little heart out touching my shoulders briskly at first before tapping me into the room. The carpet is dark blue and there is a little narrow bed with a dresser headboard. Some of the Ziploc bags traveled to rest on the bed leaving me to believe that this is all I own. What I wonder is in those bags? I walk over to the bed pulling the bags open and dumping them out onto the bed. Birdie sweetly slows her chirp and pulls open a dresser drawer. There is another robe, more socks with the little rubbery stickers and 3 pairs of drawstring pants everything in a pale blue. I don't know what I am hoping for as I hold up each one putting the soft cloth on my face before putting it into Birdie's expectant hand hovering over the bed. The sweet slow song she sings sounds sorrowful and I watch her face for tears. I watch her as she finishes the last short note. Her face is dry her make-up perfect and she turns leaving the room with the door open.

       He would sleep in the bed with me leaving the door open into the hallway. I was still tied to the bed wrists crossed left over right with a long lead to the front post under the mattress. I could touch my face with the palm of my right hand feel my lips held in place by cotton thread. As I lay on my side facing the door his slow breath across my shoulder I would drift off to sleep. I pull the little bed over to the far wall making the dresser the foot I snug it to the wall. I turn looking out my open door at the women leaning on the hallway wall. The nurses are gathering them up their voices little notes as they shuffle their light blue limbs out of the hallway to the couches. I stand there at my door I turn my head further down the hallway where I have not gone.

There are several doors on both sides of the hallway all of them closed. As I step into the hallway I fan out my fingers on the door pushing it as I look left. The door flattens onto the hallway wall opposite the nurses desk on the far side of the lounge where the women are all turned facing me. A nurse clears her throat and each woman turns her back towards the TV against the back wall. Leaving the door open I step back into my room laying down on the bed where I can see out the door I put my shoulders against the wall. It's cold immobile and silent as I sink my weight into it. My bed with him had travelled from the center of the room to the corner he would climb over me getting in and out of bed more often though he would dragged me in and resting his weight on me he would sleep. I would sleep. Waking to him sitting on the bed pinching my ass cheek. I began to wait for each pinch staying perfectly still until he slid the needle out. My legs twitch in the bed as I rub where my IV most recently delivered comfort. Birdie appears in the doorway a little tray with two cups these blue and white pills singing the same slow tune as she rests them on the dresser. Sitting up she hands both cups to me and I throw back the pills and water I give her the pill cup and hold the water one up. My lips are dry and I'm so thirsty. She sweetly chirps taking the tray and returning with a larger glass and a pitcher of water I trade the glasses drinking the cool water steady until it's empty Birdie wraps her hand around mine and the glass pouring while she chirps after she sets the pitcher down she takes ointment off the tray and paints my lips. Holding out her arms she sighs before taking the tray and leaving me sitting on the bed.

It's a relief the cold, the cold pills and even the dark blue walls. It smells of absence. I miss his scent. The curl of his fingers around my ribs. His voice the way he would sigh in his sleep and I know there is more but I find myself torn. How can I go on without his heartbeat filling up my skull? Without the taste of him or the feel of him? Now it's only me every moment in every breath. He was a jealous man accusing me of past lovers searching for me. That some day there would be a knock at the door and one of my exes would bust down his door. He would untie me and shout at me pushing me into the living room slapping me if I took a step. I would lean on the nearest wall putting both hands flat and spreading my limbs out. He would go silent rubbing the marks along my limbs then licking them he would pull me down to the floor and tell me over and over again all mine. His hand on my shoulders pinning me down to the wood my arms sprayed out in front of me he would take me slamming my hips into the wall after he was done before dragging me back to my bed by my foot. He would tell me how no one would ever find us. They wouldn't be looking because no one knows but us. They wouldn't understand a love like ours. They would be jealous and keep us apart. You should hope they never find us. He would pant as he would beat me using the belt laying me over the bed bound as if in prayer. He would collapse belt hitting the floor and lay there panting the rhythm of his breathing evening out, he would look me in the eye before knocking me out.

I sit up in the narrow bed the door clicking closed I stumble out onto the carpet crawling then standing I grasp the handle and push the door open to the empty hallway glowing a glassy blue. The silence stands firm as I turn to look down each side empty chairs and closed doors but not a person in sight. My bare feet on the tile turn blue with my steps. I inspect the lounge touching the couches and patting the chairs. The couch is plastic maybe old vinyl but barely supple it's metal arms painted blue the seats now faintly blue. I'm not wearing the robe while the drawstring pants feel worn and soft the shirt is a new white cotton still package creased. I tug at the collar. Lay down on the tile my head cement dripping out my pores. I can hear footsteps, I can hear his breath slapping me in the face. One cheek then the other waves quivering melting under his fingers. It's too much my heart feels crushed in his teeth. My devoured body gives way listening to the stop. I hear my breath hard punching into an ounce of lung. My heart bursts and I let the hot droplets leak out into the cold tile floor as I draw each breath slow and patient through my open mouth. I'm still on the floor, I'm still warm with heart even broken. I feel the tears dripping down my face I sigh looking for vowels but find only mist on the floor. I lay there on my side next to the biggest couch draining into numbness.

I wake up in the little narrow bed, Birdie singing throwing her shoulders back she has two white cups and offers them to me. I toss back the pills chasing it with the lonely sip of water. I want everything to go down as easily, I want to swallow everything I know. I lay there in the narrow bed watching out the open door as the pale blue women gawk at me. When their eyes meet mine they look away and scatter from the door. It's quiet even as Birdie drifts over the floor into the hallway.

I lay there trying to leak out my pores, settling into the spreading warmth of the sheets. I can feel his hands down my sides pushing his fingers into the hollows of my ribs searching for gaps and bones. Every inch he runs his fingers his hands and even his lips, I am a lead weight, a metal slug pouring myself into my bones. I sweat out my breath feel the temperature drop inside me. Then slip out my skin drowning in the dew of each morning. I can't stand the sun and hold my breath at first light whimpering as the ray slips over my face in the narrow bed. This day and Birdie with her tray no pills in the cups no prick of a needle I can't hear her as she takes my arm to stand me her mouth is open belting out but nothing reaches me. Double white sits behind his desk pen and papers tapping a blue pen between his fingers. The throb of my heart begins to pace before I slump over in the chair. I'm under water in the bath tub looking up at him, the bubbles lingering at my lips. His gorgeous eyes a pale grey as he pulls me up to the surface slaps me and returns my head to the bottom of the tub face up. His thumb in my throat his other fingers fanned out over my neck. Water up the sides of the tub as he steps in to hold me down I can see the sky blue and not a single cloud. Hear my heart freight train as my breath explodes on the surface eye to eye with his slippery blue irises. My hands aren't bound and I slip them around his throat pushing him out of the tub and losing to gravity the tile floor slaps my first breath before he rolls me under him palming my head licks my lips and panting fucks me loudly pressing my hips into the floor and I throb. Wait for breath or for empty sleep. I hear a TV. I feel that needle pop rushing my heart rate before a loud sigh sweeps away my quivering jelly. His lips at my ear I hear him say he loves me and until death will we part. I can't be without you, will not live another day with out your skin on mine. Without the sweet taste of your flesh, I would rather die here now in your arms.

But life is never so perfect. That is never the end of life simply one story. One famed moment where our hearts weep before slowing to steady. The tapping of a nurses shoes stops at my bed side. A little bird not nearly as sweet shakes my shoulder and I squint her big sad eyes and doll drawn mouth look a little surprised as I widen my lids turning my blue eye to her as I rise out of bed. She hesitates then gathers up my clothes and strips the bed. I stand there feeling a smile slip across my face. The nurse turns her flat song cut short as she pats me down before sighing to finish the verse. I hear Double white march down the hallway and I measure his steps. Hearing them stop at the open door I turn as two men gather me up. No my future has never been certain and I prefer to hope for mercy then to get over wrought about the sour parts. Double white walks behind and at the elevator a wheel chair

stands empty. My feet barely reach the floor
and seated I lean back resting on the leather. In
and out of the elevator and into a silent hall,
double white unlocks one door Birdie is not
here and neither is Doll. It's a narrow little
room with a proper hospital bed with upper arm
restraints. They strap me in and put a leather
strip across my chest before Doll appears with
an IV pole. She taps my inner right elbow as
Double white tells me that this is for my own
safety. They will be stepping me off the
morphine. He closes the file and Doll writes
down the time from her watch and then empties
a syringe into my tubing. Hanging the
clipboard on the door Doll locks me in and
through the glass in the door I can see her nod
before following Double white.

There are no birds here. I lay my head
down closing my eyes. It's warm and sweet
much sweeter than before, the leather around
my upper arms is soft and smells of antiseptic.
I broke in brown leather thigh cuffs on the
hardwood floor of the living room. I wore
them in the living room from then on. He
would listen to music and leave welts across
my thighs. Often fucking me after each beating
with a flat leather belt. At first the thick straps
would cut into my skin but soon they softened
smelling of salt, blood and sex. I can hear
piano as I hold my ear to the floor boards then

wake up in the bed strapped in as Doll tops my
dreams off. She looks into my eyes then
scratches down a few words before tapping her
thin little ankles out the door. I take a deep
breath drawing up my chest filling the vacancy
along each rib until the throb is slowed. Letting
out the air listening to ticks of a wall clock. I
want him layered on my skin dragging me out
of this future without sound or fury. It wells up
and each sigh has not brought any sound to my
lips. What would change? It seems the whole
of everything has changed turning my empty
thoughts into millions of fleeing atoms. No
longer sticky or coated in my own flesh I am
lost adrift in a space beyond his touch. Beyond
anyone's touch for that matter. Nothing hurts
me here and nothing occupies me in this
loneliness. Even the cotton clothing hangs off
the disappearing pulp of me. Am I drawing
myself away? Trying to escape these washed
out needs. I am snug in the leather but every
other inch is free.

       What good is freedom to a broken
heart? He read to me passages from dog eared
paperbacks sometimes lapsing into silence for
hours before reading another word. The spines
were soft and nipped as he would slip it into his
back pocket before flipping me onto my back
or side to tightened my bounds. Doll fingers
the buckles slipping her finger between the

leather and my chilled skin her nail polish perfectly smooth dragging the blanket edge up my shoulders, she leans over while pulling the chair under her nearer to the bed. I smell perfume a lemon sweet pungent mouthful my mouth waters as I lick my lips Doll sighs switching ankles before her hand comes to rest on my face. Her palm is dry on my cheek. My skin feels buttery on the pads of her fingers stroking my cheek she sighs again letting her lips part to exhale. The slippery rubber of my veins as I turn my head to look up but the leather at my shoulder allows not an inch. Colder as I hear Doll stand up her voice serenading me a saxophone drifting beyond my nose. He's ripe and bursting as my heart floods out I feel the static zip of the paddles drawing up the shock. It's thunder in the desert so far from the throb of light tracing out my mouth I cling for air only to pop sending me outside my breath I hear Double white barking over the hiss. But then I am left with the ripe smell of him. The sharp pining to feel my lips on his as I swell pushing air out trying to void my own lining.

I can see the floor spread out beneath me listening to the wail of guitars and the ping of the strap. The muscles in my chests are thick holding me one shoulder to wood with my face half resting on grain. There is fight in my thighs trembling after each stroke. It is Doll wiping my face with soft cotton as I open my eyes and I let out my sigh quivering my lower lip letting it rest as Doll sets down the wash cloth to slip her first finger over my healing lips. First the bottom then the top she uses the corner of the cloth to clean the lingering ointment from the raised edges where the thread pushed through and across holding my mouth together. Her own lips painted a bright red as she holds them in a pucker fixed on my face she pauses to sigh settling back into the chair. Her serenade becomes flat the sultry slip of her voice as the breathy song fills the room, I close my eyes.

My own thoughts return the hammering words of inquisition. I think about the bright grocery store floor, shelf after shelf of illuminated boxes. His body turning as he saw me, my heart chattering in my chest as I drew near each time to his flesh. Then I feel hollow cold beneath the weight of my heart. Doll is beautiful to look at and I close my blue eye turning my head to gaze. The nice wooden chair she sits ramrod, the edges worn and polished silky with her porcelain skin, her lips stay closed as she pours over the magazine in her lap. The turn of the fresh pages her finger under the unseen reading lips puckered. A tide of whispers crests I hear their buzz and fail to know the words. His lips on my ear licking the upper cartilage while pausing to announce my ill gotten joy from each moment spent together. I know the sound of a vowel sometimes mashed in his jowls. When summer seeped into the air my skin wept out my scent staining his life. Then with tears in his eyes he slapped me yelling in tirade after tirade that who would understand. Who could live this way unable to love? You will never leave my side only together are we whole. His words hung there as I lay trussed up in a narrow bed. I leaked his love through my pores trying to sweat out the tingles of each needle. Doll stroked my face her nails tracing my hair line, she smelled sweet leaning over me bruising her bosom against my shoulder. My nasty breath draws out the gummy length of my veins. The blanks between my body turns short scratched with warm putty skin. Then Doll dampens my brow cooing as she bathes the dirty film from my face and neck. I feel the leather slip beneath each shoulder the buckle clanking on the rails. Doll turns me removing my torn wet shirt I have stained everything in my sticky sweat and clogged air way. Fighting until I knock all the air out of each lung, the prize and the consolation are unconsciousness. I stare up at Doll carefully draping a warm dry cotton sheet over me her hands slide over my damp skin. I

can not contain the tremors, the electric zip
rolling from follicle to follicle as I face away
from Doll's well meaning touch. As I draw up
my legs knowing I am clean of him and not one
ounce of him remains with me. My body has
wept him out in a black peel the goo with in my
bones. Without his love do I exist? The ache
as Doll brings me to stand the cold floor tile
blue I stare at my feet I see my wet breath. Out
the window of the door I see a face wearily
watching the faded brown eyes unconcerned
with me seeing them. Doll turns me and I can
see a reflection of my side in the bathroom
door. Under my left breast a small square of
cotton is carefully taped I draw up my chest
filling my rib cage as I bare my left side and
tear the bandage off. My right hand pauses
beneath raised edges of his brand. I can smell
sweat as he burned them slapping and spitting
but before he crushed the wound with ink he
licked my smoldering side. I'm panting, Doll's
arms laying me on the floor as I hear his voice
split the air. I collapse before the ground meets
me. The birds caw crackling as I mumble hear
the low grain of my voice and slip my right
hand over his pride of ownership. Who would
love you as completely as I? You wouldn't be
alive without my love. His hands often traced
my ribcage standing in the kitchen my hands
spread out on the counter in front of me. There

won't be another after me because I am the only one who will love you. You are the only one that loves me. He turned me around to face him my hands full of his pecks. Tell me you love me. He would slap me then tell me how I can't say it even if my lips weren't sewn shut. He said I didn't have a heart to love him, that I stayed because I feared him. He threw me at the door kicking me up against the door frame. I would stand there and place my hand on the door watching him. From a small drawer he would take a gun and point it at me. I would let go of the door knob and turn toward the wall facing him cheek to the wallpaper. The tip of the barrel felt warm turning me to face him the barrel in my ribs I would drop to the floor and rest my temple there at the opening. He pulled the trigger a dull click then put the gun back in the drawer only feet from the front door. Dragging me down the hallway he would tie me to the bed and sit watching me from the plain wooden chair.

Doll slips her chair forward to tap my IV, her perfume blended with nicotine. Then begins lifting my shoulders out of the leather restraints by tilting me right pressing her firm hands along my back to loosen the strap between my shoulders. I can smell the wet leather and it chokes me of air and I sit up startling Doll as she drops the strap sending the

buckles dragging across my soft left shoulder.
I let out a heavy sigh as little red tares weep
Doll braces me sitting me at the edge of the bed
resting my weight against her shoulder. I can
hear the ocean slosh in my stomach feel a
pounding wave land pushing me into the bed.
Doll rolls me to my side as the ocean leaves
me. The stark birds cry their hard gulp of air
my own I can not contain so much my heart
fills my chest crushing my bones in my skin.
Then the sky opens up and rolling rain down
my face, I am the thunder the silken threads of
night. My mouth is cotton filled and thickly
filmed. I'm looking for a letter all I have is M.
Doll takes the wash cloth to my face, stroking
my lips then brushes my teeth inspecting then
with a tap from the flat of the brush. She takes
me to the sink in the bathroom and motions for
me to rinse handing me a cup I smell and then
fill my mouth with cold antiseptic the spit turns
the sink pink and Doll has me sit on the closed
toilet while she steps out closing the door
behind her and I am now faced with my
reflection. I shift putting both feet together and
drawing up my weight onto the edge I stand put
out one hand to lean on the door and pull my
shirt up to stare an my left side. I hold my
breath inching the flat of my palm against the
brand. All mine I say to the mirror my blue eye
clear and crisp as I step back to rest on the

toilet the door swings in Doll brought a grey coated doctor he uses a flashlight to poke his gloved fingers along my tooth line. I lay my open jaw on the sink edge as the doctor takes out a chart and taking notes taps them one by one he says nothing, the sound of his pen and rubber fingers become slow static. He gathers up his notes and tosses the gloves from his hands as Doll ushers me into a waiting wheel chair.

Down the hall we go and the smell of life wells up into my nose I fill my chest from the last trace of Doll's perfume on my shoulder. But the sound of mirth squeezes my heart and although I have both hands over my mouth I scream through them putting my head in my lap as the light of day strikes me from an open window. Doll stops the wheels and crouching before me tries to sit me up and pulling my legs into the chair I turn and climb over the leather back tumbling to the floor my moist hot breath rising from the floor as an orderly restrains me. Wiping the blood and tears from my face Doll doesn't look down at the men putting cotton leg irons quieting around each ankle. On ward now bound in the chair for my own safety Doll sweetly whispers as she soothes me before topping off the new IV. I feel the light hear the white noise of the hospital. Draped over another chair I can see him touching my cheek his blue eyes white I paw at the air but each hand is not responding and he slips away in the band of red light. My mouth is full of cardboard but I found an A gnawing at my ear. The chill of my veins silences my sweating heart. I long to be with him.

To hear him sleeping next to me with the birds chirping to have no need to speak or think or even feel. To be the gloom of night wet on the dawn's grass. I slump over held in the chair by the cotton ties let the cardboard hit the cream tiles and push that hard A from my chest. Rolling my shoulders I slam back into the chair and then fling myself forward leading head first, Doll rushes into the room her voice cooing while she tenderly wipes the sweat off my face I can see her eyes pleading with me and after tightening my bounds she coaxes another cardboard film into my mouth this time holding my face to let the doctor finish the x-rays.

Doll keeps repeating various letters pausing to see if I respond. She pushes me back to the deep blue room where at least it's dim and quiet. Before opening the door she forms her mouth into a slow 'home' smiling before flipping the door open. I don't see any shoulder restraints Doll removes the IV and warming her hands continues the alphabet while applying lotion to my hands, arms and legs. A little song follows her as she tucks the sheet around me and once again rests in the plain wooden chair beside the narrow bed. Falling silent hands rested in her lap as she leans in and covers my blue eye before kissing my forehead. My nose at her throat her heart beat warming the sweet perfume as I close my eyes.

I know there is always a before and after. There is always a breath before and one after. My mind doesn't see before and I am laying here in the after. I want to allow myself there to be nothing before I arrived here. The scent of Doll hangs over my skin as she looms over the bed. I open my eye and it's an open window with a stiff cold breeze. The room is empty and the door is closed. I am not bound to the bed or tethered by an IV, so I stand up letting the bedding fall as I slip to the window sill. The moon is pale dulling the stars with streaks, I'm cold standing naked resting over the sill, hands pushing up the sash. Only six inches and less than one foot wide but it's the view a few floors from the street that brings my arms in and I close the window afraid the wind might taunt me. I turn and slip back into the cool sheets, laying there I listen for the sounds of life. I suck my breath and hold it, feel the shake of my chest and cough it out. Resting my right hand under my left breast I finger a raised scar.

He's in the kitchen I heard the gas ignite and smelt the high lick of the flame. Tied to a plain wooden chair my chest thrust out and shoulders braced over the back, I am swallowing my breath, passing out and slapped into breath again. He's licking my face excited running his mouth down my ribs. Pulling back to send the heavy leather belt across my left side. Show me your heart he screams show me it's mine. Leaning in close he whispers show me your love chewing my ear. I fill up puffing out as he presses the sizzling metal against my left lung. The whole of sound collapses I lull head backward the ceiling a dinghy white the silence pure and swelled by my heart. Loud slap beats flopping each stroke of my thorax the leather sweats and his spit stains my inner cavity. His voice cracks the wood as I tumble to the floor still pressed to the grain my heart gasps stalling in the surrender of my breath. My eyes are open and I'm watching him fuck me wrapping a hand around my neck to lick the burning flesh. It is the pop of his tears down my face as he slaps air into my lungs. I fill up my chest my heart splattering hot lava down my belly. He sobs wailing as he lifts me over his shoulder and fills the tub with my bones. The dark blood smeared on his face down his chest as he turns the water on and gets into tub with me. Stroking my hair putting my hands in my lap as he sits me up to adjust the temperature. His humming rests my split chest, I exhale taking in the scent of his exposed skin. The flat of his chest settled against my back as he washes the blood from our bodies. The still of the salt scrub twinges the bath water. He puts words to the melody, cooing his voice low and nestled in my ear.

The drip of the faucets becomes the rap of Det. Nervous notebook silenced as he clicks his pen. I'm sitting up Double white stands on one side as another doctor and Det. Nervous face him over my bed. "her dental x-rays are all the help we can give you since you already have her finger prints and DNA. " He holds his fingers up two of them. Det. Nervous clears his throat. "Can you tell me your name?" I run my hand under my shirt smiling as he shifts his weight. "Can you speak?" The A comes out hard as I rise up over my ankles standing in the bed pulling my shirt off to cup my breast and thump the scar he put there. Det. 's mouth comes open and Double white pushes a big button on the wall bringing Doll and Birdie in to subdue me as the men turn away hands over their eyes. Their shame appeared after the nurses rubbed past them their hands sliding up my muscle threaded bones where only moments before the men had gazed. Doll lays the cold swab on me slamming my heart into longer beats anticipating the prick of a wet needle. Her hands become cold as I roll into the injection the men still lingering at the door. I feel my mouth open and Birdie slips her hands under my jaw rolling me to my side in the bed.

Soft silence strips the world of every twitch but I can still hear a buzzing, a rattling of my joints, and the shaking of my hands. His absence has drained me but my heart sighs. I rub my empty flat palm across the cream sheets slipping my fingers over the edge and down the side to the front post looking for a coil of rope. The cold metal whines under my finger. My right hand drifts across my face tracing my lips, my teeth as I spread my lower lip and bite my palm to still my digits. My breath is hard rolling H as I sit up in the bed legs in front of me and back against the wall at the top of the bed. The wooden chair is pushed up against the wall empty. Filled with moon light the floor glows dull hot on my feet as I step out of bed chest over heels to touch the seat of the chair. I smell the splits in the grain where it dips and the shine smooth back. Antiseptic I draw up standing over the chair hands open the thin gown tied in the back. I draw up my nostrils' flare out with the huff and fling the chair at the wall until it lays down surrendering on the floor, I hold my breath putting both hands over my mouth. Waiting I stand still over the bits of chair when an orderly Velcro faced flings open the door. "get in bed" he whispers propping open the door he brings in a trashcan and broom with dustpan. "it's 3 am get in bed." He tidies the sheets and draws them open for me before offering me his hand. My upper lip quivers and I hear heels down the hallway I turn my head to watch a tall thin nurse stride into the open door. "clean this up" she waves her fingers over the wooden chair and takes me under the armpits clearing her throat she presses her fingers into my ribs as I let her push me to the bed, turn and sit before tucking me in and with a firm hand she rubs my back humming. I watch the orderly sweep up the chair depositing every chunk in the garbage as he takes the broom and it with him closing the door after him. I lay there wide eyed listening to a faint heart sniffle feeling weight push down my shoulder. I can't watch the dull cream rise of the pillow while I hear the nurse cautiously swing the door as she escapes back into the hallway.

       I can hear him whispering in my ear his lips resting on the turned curve. It smells rotten as his flesh becomes cold settling through my lungs, my breath hangs by my nostrils. "you still belong to me" his hands slips up my throat and turning my head he kisses me pulling my jaw open. Biting my lips drawing out air his finger turns my carp mouth back to the bed. My hard in take of air pushes me over the bed and onto the floor. I lay there on the chilled blue tile staring under the bed. I begin to weep flatting my hands out on the tile. I can't see his face. His voice is quiet in my head now whispering scarcely forming words. I can still smell the gun on my hand drawing my right hand into my mouth I use my first two fingers to tap my teeth and with my cheek flatten I clear my throat coughing then silent. What does my voice sound like? His voice soothed me. Deep and rippled with small crackles, I could listen to him talk for hours. Did I ever have anything to say? What word would be important enough to say first? What life will I have now that his is over? Shadows stretch under the door as the night passes I'm still laying beside the bed when Doll opens the door I hear her heels steady and then slowed until her perfume drifts over me. I turn over as her hand slips under my shoulder she smiles letting me stay laying on the floor while she makes my bed as she draws back the sheet Birdie arrives with a tray. I slip into the bed as Doll tucks me in and preps my left hand where Birdie fills my vein with the warmth of lucidity.

The song Birdie sings scrolls into a love story I've heard it fill his mouth. My heavy heart rank in my chest pauses only to sway with melody. His lips thin soft spread out as he wraps them in the words of sorrow and remorse. As he strokes my soul turning his face the quiver in his rasp he clears his throat stealing my breath. The hot tears on my face are not as sweet as when he streaks me with his violence. Then embeds each morsel in the volumes between my bones. I'm carrying us both inside that dull blue eye. I close my left lick my lips still hearing him singing a snarky smile in the silence. The dull lingering silence of the dark blue room rustles taking a hard breath I get out of bed and open the door into his house. In the kitchen doorway he stands as I run my hand over my lips I rest my weight halfway into the living room. The separate thick wet sides of my mouth open as I smile before putting my finger to my lips.

It is that pain of speech becoming stones weighing down a life led in desperation. What would you have me do? Open my tongue to cry weakly he seduced me with death. Courted the hollow of my soul by draining every good intention away. A crooked girl starved with shallow ideals. I am drawn to my destruction to keep me from the misery of chance. The chances of leading a safe bitter life filled with the paces of school then adulthood to produce and rear intolerable heartaches whom will follow into the madness someday joining you in the earth. Death is never side stepped. Loves anything but know that everything dies. Why not love death? I could gorge myself on the tentative follies and still not have enough gravity to flee the orbit. I shed any ounce not willing to take the chance on love, on the unknown sensations of death. I showed him my fierce little teeth smelled decay on his hands. My heart beats faster nothing to hold my mouth. My hands at my sides my lips curling into a smile as he crosses into the living room. The intense throb of my organs stabs out from my left breast cutting my air empting both lungs.

It's Doll slapping my face and as I open my eyes her mouth forms an O while a black line crawls her cheek. Her startled cry drawing two orderlies in. The shoulder restraints return and both men quickly buckle me down exchanging looks between coordinated hands. I hear the rolling wheels of a trolley and see the heart monitor as Birdie bolts it to the wall before sitting on the edge of the bed to apply the leads. Her eyes don't meet mine she tilts her head down before she stand she swallows a dry K. Double white rolls a chair in and his clipboard in lap begins to mouth words which I only see his lips moving I'm hearing static crawling over the walls. Little snapping beads of sweat pour over my body as I hear the amps concentrate into a flat dull pitch. An epicenter from my hearts hole has rolled my flesh out I yield soft fading into the slap.

He's looking down at me his eyes whitely blue his mouth open I feel his hand slam flat across my face my jaw slack and bounce. I can't look back letting my right eye close against the wood while my left stares at his ankle. The inner rise of his instep as he steps closer before kneeling down to straddle me. I can't look him in the eye as he palms my jaw. Can this not be lost in the sea of my pounding heart? The electric zip turns I can smell a fire in my loins. If I give in maybe everything will stop? Maybe my heart won't accept defeat.

Doll sits on the edge of the bed the washcloth cold in her hands dripping across crisp white sheets covering my lily white chest. The tips of her manicured nails scratching until I sigh letting the static out in huffs between her paws as she leans in to stain my forehead. It's my inability to let my fingers rest rolling the sheets between lose folds trying to surface. The blanket of white padding and dusted edges of my arm I lay back my head closing my eyes.

I can smell Doll's perfume against the cotton blanket hear a fan rustle the curtain. I turn freely resting each shoulder into the pillow. A sweet summer night has awakened me sitting up I examine my legs, arms and hands. Sweating through the thin gown I lay it over the bed as I stand naked at the open door to a washroom. A full mirror on the door shows me all of my parts together. One hand shoves the door further open leaning on the mirror I see my ghostly skin in the harsh fluorescent light. Standing up I finger the scars along my chest looking around the bathroom I find grey scrubs sitting out. I lick the little red punctures on the back of my hand. Sitting on the bathroom floor alien white coated in dull grey I am a lump of flesh misshapen while surviving the torrents. Through such destruction I chiseled my body without thought of future or present. It didn't occur to me that I might live beyond my misfortunes. I only entertained the darkest of blues and the rawest of my emotions. Drank up fear by soaking in its rush. I charmed the monster by begging him to kill me. Take me from all the madness I can no longer contain my violent heart.

It's late in the night but I can hear crickets through the thick cement walls. I'm not sure where I'm at or even where I have been. Time as always doesn't run concurrent in my memories. I hear a boy calling me over the ripple of the running few inches of creek through my sneakers. Walking down the rocks to get under the street bridge I stand on the sand island around the concrete center pylon. Sunset is glowing in the street lamps over the road twisting across the slow bend of creek.

The arching current opens my eyes as double white mouths again before silencing the birds. A nasty crow looks head side to side from the crook of the street lamp while I stand on his porch. I open my mouth as the crow caws shoving its beak out. Lifting my chest as I held out my arms the crow spreads out his wings baring his black chest at me. His hard cawing a murder of crows tightening into each shriek, The slamming of doors hinges well oiled I am running after my heart. A thick trail down the dark blue floor as Doll drags her heels in the swinging of her hips. Her lips pucker she is offering me water, offering me relief, and neither seems to still my hands. They lay in my lap while I sit on the couch the TV static a grainy green. I turn them over to find my palms symmetrical. Then the length of each finger compared left to right, I see my hands in the TV glass and lay each down to try and form my face. I hear nothing. I am engulfed in a blissful unknowing paralyzed lips. My hand over my mouth I feel the heat of my breath. Then palm down to find my pulse under my rib cage. Still alive but where have my thoughts gone? Still flesh as I run my hand under the thin scrubs to rub the bones of my shoulder the muscle lean coating ribs. The cloth is heavy I tug on the neckline and then slip my fingers through my short plush mane letting it fall over my hand before cradling my aching head between both palms. I can smell Doll on my wrists then clinging to the chest of my shirt. It's layered well but not his I stand take off the shirt but look up to see an orderly mouth open coming towards me. A blanket is thrown over me and the warmth of the wave buckles my knees.

Face down on the wood living room floor I pick myself up and stand facing him taking my right hand to my mouth before backhanding him. He returns the slap then turns me by my shoulder to sweep me back down to the floor. The huff of his breath as he licks my stung face. Tying my hands behind me he runs his fingers under my hips to lift them up. I rest my weight on my knees folded in front of him. His mouth, the edge of his teeth running down my back while his hand pinches my ass cheek. I surrender my mouth liquid down to my toes the strokes of his palms ripples in a tranquil pool. He calls to me tells me how I make him want until he feels he will burst. That the over ripe swell of his love for me has ruined him forever. I am all that he needed. I wasted his time because we should always have been together. He wants to make sure we will never part to make up for it. Together he says you and I forever as he cries over the slap of the leather on my thighs. Slamming me onto my side he unties me to lick my wrists the raising welts on my upper arms and thighs. Then taking my face in his hands he tells me how the world will not understand our love and we will always have to be a secret. That I don't need the sun. Don't need anything if I can't have you.

I wake up to a darkness velvet in my mouth before I lift my bones I feel the weight of his hand resting on my back. I'm laying there uncovered twisted but not tied in the sheets. Drawing my elbows under my ribs I turn to gaze at his pale smooth face the little scar not so much an imperfection but a warning. Turning my hips I slip his hand onto the bed and flatten my body against the bed stare at the ceiling. It's silent as I strain to hear past my heart beat. His hand rests over my heart fingers rubbing the valley under my breasts. Then flat over the cleft between he spreads his fingers and gathers me into his arms resting his chin over my shoulder. His body is cold, damp and his tongue ice in my ear I run my hands over my thighs my hands shaking the right one steady panting while I hold my breath. Not one word as he lays his body over me holds my hands over my head and fills me with violent spasms. I feel the cold pull out my organs. I let my breath go as he slips his thumb into my mouth. I feel my icy limbs tangle with his the throb of my heart slowing until it stops. It's a loud zap crinkling up a fiery smell.

I'm holding the gun to his chest the trigger clicks but it's not loaded, I squeeze it again. He smiles arms at his sides. I back hand him the gun still in my hand my lip tugged up. Blood on his lips still smiling as he strips the gun from my hand kissing me smearing the blood down my throat to lick my chest. On his knees he grabs my ankles slamming my backside onto the floor. I close my eyes. I fight not to suck a hard breath or taste the blood in my mouth. I feel fingers across my face. An oxygen mask plastic air as I flinch under the restraints. Death is easy. There's nothing easy about love. My heart ruptures filling my lungs with molten air.

A tiny beep stabs me above my right eye causing my lid to twitch. I open my mouth turning on my side to let out the fumes and watch my breath barrel out. The stillness of the blue room now broken by the tiny persistent beep of what must be a cordless heart monitor.

The shapeless gown ties behind my shoulders I throw back the sheet to the end of the bed seeing the covers on the dark tile piled up on one side. Sitting up I use my fingers to examine my face, my lips and my teeth to be sure. I sit there leaning my nearly naked back on the stone wall at the head of the bed. It's chilly but my skin is faintly blue toughen by the scar tissue. His scar tissue a trail slipping into every memory. There is nothing else running through me not even my blood only thoughts of the little tremble of his lower lip before he would back hand me hard enough to turn my head but not hard enough for me to not turn towards him again. To look into his murky grey eyes the faint odor of deodorant engulfed in cinnamon I can't taste him but the cinnamon is so strong I can taste it. Here in this far away place without him day after day. I'm still not sure how long a day is or how the night ends. Where the pale of my dreams brings or leaves me. I stroke the sheets sitting there listening to silence. I can't hear his voice, I close my eyes thinking of his face and although I recall his blonde faint stubble it's all silence. There are no birds. Not here in the blue where my hands look thinner than I remember and my veins throb up through my skin. I'm still pale not a milky white but an olive blush. I run my fingers through the silk slip of hair growing a few inches from my skull. I roll my fingers down feeling where my neck juts out of my shoulders. My collar bone juts out but I can still cup my hand around one breast, the nipple tender. Sitting up straight before laying down to rest my hands under my head my left hand over my mouth I slide my right under my left breast the skin hangs over my ribs rippled only where I am branded. It makes me sigh roll over onto my back to rest my left over my right. Then the left pushes the right centering my hands over my ribs. I count my ribs letting my lips loosen. I put my big toes side by side I line up my body as I would imagine him in a coffin. Laid out still silent perhaps he still lays in a morgue drawer the fate of his body undecided.

I can't find myself any faith. There is no one to ask. No one in here but me. I'm not frightened. I take a deep sigh I can't resist death. I can't fake the thrill of living. I can't fake anything every bone has been exposed and even the cordless heart monitor must cry out to someone. The weight is like a sticker on my sternum. There is a scalloped edge I trace it out using my nail to try to scrape one up I try each finger on my right hand my thumb the most useless. It's not what I'm thinking about, it's the smell of antiseptic as I imagine myself laid out on the slab. My cold shoulders flat against the metal, I hold my breath still my heart, slow it down as I allow my body temperature to drop. I faced death every minute for months, was prepared to roll over in my grave and eat dirt. Up and then down my chest rises as I can not stop my organs. But there is still silence, I know there must be words. Words I can fill my mouth with to clear the thoughts from my head. I'll always think of him no matter how little of him I remember. It' what I'm not thinking about, my survival in this blue room. The crisp sheets and blankets piled on the floor while I stand to walk a few steps. The door is only feet away but I can't grasp what might lay behind it. Put my hand on the handle rest it there as I lay my cheek to the door listening closing my eyes. I take a deep hard breath then lean against the door, palms flat avoiding the thin long rectangular window. I pound the door as if each stroke were my heart beat I use both hands and they curl into fists as my breath quickens. Filled with the dum-dum of my rhythm it's the scream that erupts from my chest that stops me.

You always hurt the ones you love. There are splinters under my nails while I claw the surface of the door until Doll opens it followed by two orderlies. I stand calm as she takes my arm leading me onto the bed where I lay down as she injects me. Her lips move but nothing stains my silence she shakes out the sheets and blanket. The whole of the world may not exist when I close my eyes. There's nothing to prove the morning will come. I know it will even in this long drawn night. I can smell Doll as she sits on the bed her hand caressing my face. Her thumb traces the orb of my right eye then my ear lobe. Her fingers warm as she slips them under the edge of the gown onto the scalloped edged sticker. Doll's hands were warm, the scent of her porcelain glow drooped my lids as I could hear violins moan her bosom heaved as she sang to me. The chords silky as her hands and opening my mouth only strings came out. I groaned her lips made me think of blood. My hot mouth gaping open, her head as she sings out tilting, swaying in time, slipping my stomach as I fought for consciousness. She leaned over kissing my forehead brushing her chest across my hands and arms.

On the floor I was sucking a breath on all fours coughing up my tongue wetting my lips. My right gave way onto my side I landed bracing myself with my shoulder. There's no sound as I feel the belt buckle snap my side. My heart pauses at impact only to skip a beat before marching on. Standing up I take the belt from his hands and slap his face. He slaps me I let my head rest on my left shoulder. Turning my head I stare into his grey eyes. I feel a quiver that begins in my right hand. I back hand him stepping closer and follow with the belt only to fall forward. It's Doll's smell that makes me open my eyes. The weight of her hand over my sternum. Her polished nails digging into my left breast before gliding over his brand. Her eyes meeting mine as she lulls me with her fingertips. Blood red lips turned up ward as each word must weigh nothing. I can no longer tell if she's singing or speaking because I'm surrounded by stunned silence. My heart turns cold when I hear it finally, a single drum then a long dash. I am overcome with its pitter patter and I close my eyes feeling an echo bring Doll's sweet lullaby into the room. For once I sleep.

I smell a sweet wet stench coating my skin I'm cold and Doll's warm hand caresses the hollow of my shoulders. Lying on my face her fingers travel down my jaw bone slipping around my neck and over my left shoulder. Petting me stroking the cold hollows her comfort feels fake. Shush I hear her whisper it's alright now. Shush I hear the birds, hear him singing I can't place where I have heard the tune, his lips curl up and he turns his back to me as he washes a plate. The flat of his palm keeps time on the counter then he stands facing me in the kitchen. A warm glow from the window behind him softens the edges of his shoulders as he sings louder. It is the age of his face I'm seeing, his unshaven cheek trembling in the pauses. I reach to stroke his cheek watch my fingers rest thumb under his jaw. His heart calls to me but I only want it to stop. I want to wake up. I want to never see his face. Never smell him on my skin. It's his voice telling me to choke him and those dull grey eyes welling up as I wrap my right hand around his throat. Then I run my hand down his chest pausing over his heart a loud empty note. It's my heart I heard all this time echoing in him. The swell of his chest as he clears his throat. My left hand is over my mouth I trace my lips the threads no longer there but sealed in place. There is no other word more important than any other. Freedom is a mentality not a construct. I will never be free of him. I cover my right eye taking my hand off his chest. Enfolded in his arms it is Doll's soft lip that interrupts. A flute piping into my ear while her hand rubs my shoulders. I can't bear her charity, her affection any longer but I can't do anything but cry. I hear my sobbing through my hand. The noise disgusts me. It's violent swift crackle as I take in a big breath and hold still. I want to be invisible. A tear instead of producing them. Something smaller than an atom. Crickets call out beyond the trees as lightening bugs hang over the grass. Lying on my back I hear the wind ruffling the blades of grass, the sweet heat of a summer's night. Honeysuckle, roses and marigolds in the air, cicadas ripping hard notes I'm listening to my heart beat. A soft clap, a breathy thud as little specks fly over my horizon into the heavens a husky voice sings serenading each bug trailing against the dense night.   Take a breath with the singer, feeling the vibration of my lips, is that my voice? The loud pop of the paddles fills my lungs. Doll's milky skin as she leans over me. her breath shallow I feel her warm fingers over my face. Shush she says only a bad dream.

Her eerie glow I open my eyes to a dull evening she leans in kissing my forehead my cheek. I'm holding my breath. Hers is soft warm as she kisses my ear whispers in my neck everything is fine now. I don't feel warm, a fine mist hangs on the air I exhale as Doll straightens up standing to tuck the blanket under my chin. Her breath rolls out as she sighs before leaving the room. What everything I wonder? Am I fine? Am I any more substance than the fog of my dreams? Than the low hanging mist over the creek in the early morning, am I going to dissipate in the harsh sun? Do I exist in the liquid of my dreams, or the damp mold of my waking hours?

I face the ceiling twitching under the weight of the blanket. My thoughts leaking, what defines a life? The swell of my lungs?

My trail of dodged realities? The escape into emptiness I can't tidy my soul. I can't claim any faith. Even love is a cruel painful kiss. These lips haven't said because who would listen should I complain about the torture of the everyday modern world. I feel the pressure of expectations mired over the ignorance. Shall I educate you in the definition of freedom? True freedom is not about the majority or the individual desires of the public. Where can I feel safe when it is my fellow man that brings hostility into my life? Must you tell me how special and different I am? Curious little monkeys picking me apart. I only have my flesh to give. This violence in my heart is a strong taste and sore from each day among the onslaught of opinions. I want to open my mouth I want all the truth to come out but I don't think a soul would believe me. This pain of existence is my drug of choice. What kind of a life have I chosen to live? Anything other than yours. Be enamored and keep your pity I with all intention chose to dare to lay my hand on death to love what could kill me. I still love the idea of it. To die in his arms, to finish my conscious moments with his voice in my veins. I long to hear him. To tell him I would do it all again.

My hands rest over my rib cage, I draw in a breath trying a letter. My lips slip over my teeth I lick them feeling the scars raised still sore. A deep sigh stirs only the sound I let my mouth fall open as I trace the right edge of his brand. I can hear him tapping my skin his breath warm as he sang. His love is deadly, his temper swift. It's everything I could have needed to wipe this heart ache over a world of peering eyes. A world thoughtlessly crushing a girl. I could give I could lay down and let death have this flesh but death wouldn't take me. He spat on my wet chest then poured vodka after licking as he ran his fingers over my thighs and pushed them into my crotch. "13" he said "not so unlucky" the alcohol seeped into my mouth as he sucked on my lips he took a swig before putting the bottle on the floor. My hands tied over my head face up on that worn bed, he inspected his work. Then with his right eye closed he covered my right eye. "I want to see what you see." His fingers stank of ointment as he painted my lips while he sang about love. Tragic, sweet and lingering his voice rippled with his upper lip. Slapping my face he took my hands from the rail and turned me over to toss me down to the floor. I landed face down flat as his foot rested between my shoulders. "lucky, how lucky could one woman be?" he brought his weight down over my back sitting astride me. "I could smell you that night I met you. I know you as I know the night itself. You will never leave me. even dead I will keep your body and toss out the rest. My prized possession beloved." He sank his teeth into my left bicep as I turned to meet his eye. I closed my right eye. Palming my face he put me into the floor again then rubbed his naked body over me rolling his hips grinding me. I thought about how the floor vibrated under me. I heard a hard popping I watched dust dance under the bed. I felt a rushing alarm rip me awake as I sat up in the narrow hospital bed. Birdie washing my face telling me "it's all better now. There, there it's all better now." Her voice a slow chirp. I lay back down watching her face as she smiles showing her teeth. My eyes trace down her chest I put my hand on the pocket over her right breast she puts her hand over mine. Her heart flutters as her face turns red she sweeps my hand off and tucks it underneath the blanket. She smiles clearing her throat. I don't believe her how would she know? Turning to leave the room she flips the light off and closes the door leaving me.

I close my eyes I open my right peer at the ceiling, squares running into brick. The air smells soft with drifting notes of smoke. I pull my hands out from the blanket smelling them. My right is the same hand cream as my left a fake lavender stripped vanilla causes each one to overpower the other. My right wrist is dry and I lick it smooth once before licking my teeth trying to clear my throat listening for a few minutes after each cough. Dry inside and out, is there life left in my body? I can survive my ruptures self inflicted or not but how do I survive the good intentions of a hypocritical world? I sigh letting it drift out to a crackle. I smile as I slip my hands under the sheets running my fingers over my torso. I want to think of him. I want to relive these wounds. It's revenge against a casually cruel world. No one sees the multitude of slights piled over the course of a life. How long can anyone bear each time they are brushed aside. It would seem an unlucky life that became lucky through survival. His musky scent the scratch of his unrest. I hear a soft moan my eyes closed. It's a drifting husk a dry crackle as I arch my back. His wet mouth sucking the welt he toughens with the flat of a wooden spoon. I can't fathom the roaring freight train of my panting I sit up shift set my elbows on my knees. Put my fingers in my mouth turning my head I look around the floor examine the blanket picking at the stitches.

      The voice scared me she sounded deep quivering moaning over her heart. A tragic slippery sad she sweeps over each syllable. I hum a few soft letters. How can I be sad I lived? But how do I continue? With all these eyes on me. Sickness, is it really sickness when the world drowns me in handicap.

I want to go back to his house lay on the floors. Arch my thighs against the tub walls holding myself up. I slide over the edge of the bed securing the gown around my back and shoulders. The door opens with a touch into the hallway the glow of the elevator but further on there is a stair case. I take the stairs crouching to check each hallway as I descend to the ground floor. The door is warm and opens squealing once and popping after I step out on to the concrete stoop. I'm barefoot and the surprised man in the white shirt and black pants takes a slow drag off his cigarette before offering me it. It's sweet I fill up my aching lungs and sit white cotton on the warm block, back resting on the door. He takes it back taking another slow and crackled drag he says "you might as well enjoy the fresh air I have to put you back in your bed be daylight." I lift my ass up the door and push onto my feet taking the stub in my fingers to suck a strong full breath I put it out spitting on my fingers before swallowing it. "don't have a damn thing to say" He takes out his keys and I run heading into a parking lot. He shouts as he tackles me sending us onto the gritty pavement. I slap his face push him my fingers on his throat.

Tucking my right shoulder into the concrete nub he slaps my bare ass as he kneels on me. I taste the blood filling my mouth. It's liquid between my thighs as I can't contain my heart as it explodes a thousand times.

I smell the sharp antiseptic as Doll's delicate fingers dab my face. Her chirp is lovely I stare blankly at her. Time ticks on I'm sure but Doll seems frozen at my bedside. Licking my lips I still taste my blood, dry bits now as Doll rubs ointment over my face. The right side met the crumbling cement, I close my eyes let my lower lip fall open as Doll slips her fingertip over my teeth counting them pausing to note on the little card resting on my right breast. All the bottom teeth then tilting my head back the top row intact without a chip, I watch her finish jotting information down. Her hair in a ponytail, skin rosy she continues to sing her eyes fixed on mine. A tear wells up slipping over her left cheek stopping to pat her face she flashes a nervous smile at me and I lurch forward violently coughing as a series of sharp pokes bends me forward further holding the bed edge as I approach the floor. The room is filled with men's voices, strapping tile, but I watch the floor where Doll's black shiny Mary Jane's tap nervously. I'm flat on my back the ceiling is melting there are hands and hands down my shoulders and thighs, flat spread out trying to contain the tide of me. Their heat smells of sweat. I vomit turning my head toward the stench.

My hands break the water surface first it burns and I pull my knees to my chest turning my face away. down I look up seeing a full sky of stars as I travel further. It's the weight of my face as I look beneath me but there's only darkness. I relax my hands floating over head I loosen my jaw and watch each bubble sail away. it's cold and my limbs defy me and begin to stroke out halting the weight. Then as the stars grow until it is the flashlight of Double white. He sits there in a plain wooden chair next to the narrow bed I'm sitting up legs draped over the side hands folded in my lap. "Don't you want to live?" He taps a yellow pencil easer on the clipboard. I lean forward to look at the paper but he sets the clipboard down on the floor while he clears his throat. "I have to continue to sedate you because it would be inhuman to restrain you. I am concerned about how you fell face first into the parking lot but more concerned with how you got out of the building. Can you tell me?" It seems like a plea. His pocket vibrates shifting the pens there. Clearing his throat he slips the phone out and checks it before bending to pick up the clipboard and exiting the room leaving the chair.

I crawl to graze my hand over the seat then trace the worn cracks polished into its grain. I breath an H a HA, I lick my lips put my hand on my left cheek and close my eyes. Cover my mouth pinch my lips and take the gown off as I stand beside the bed. I face the chair knees on the front leaning forward I grasp the back and kneel on the seat letting my toes point. Resting my bare ass on my ankles it's a long sigh that sweeps me.

To live, can I have definition? Can you be specific about the purpose and scope? His love required my life. My love required his as well. Double white fills the frame paused over his phone before his eyes meet mine. Props open the door and calls back for a nurse. Doll rushes in draping the blanket over me as she coaxes me off the chair. I stand letting her dress me and stay eyes locked with Double white. He's eyeing me his face smiling damply. I slip my lips across my teeth lick the front tooth as Doll ties my gown securing me from nudity. She sighs smoothing out the sleeves tugging the sides before retying each from the bottom to the top her hands slip over my neck and throat and I look down at her closing my left eye. Sliding me back onto the bed her hands wrap around my hips palms flat. I sigh as she combs my hair while Double white disappears.

I watch the rise of her chest imagine her heart feel her cover me with the blankets before Birdie joins us. The little tray Birdie sets on the stand the needle she taps before Doll turns my head my chin in her palm. I smile letting every tooth dry as the warmth fills my mouth. There is only sweetness despite the song Birdie sings her little lower lips trembles and a tear liberates itself from her makeup. Wiping it away she gathers up the tray taps Doll and they leave letting the door shut.

I am alone. It is haunting the silence. The ache of my face as I cry the tips of my fingers not halting the tears. Anything would fill the cavity of my chest I swell with flimsy breath. The tears stop but the silence endures I roll onto my back watch the ceiling shrink as I hold a hand toward it. I sit up the door is right there I get out of the bed where I lay beside him. I turn watch his face as he rolls onto his back I slip the sheet off me and stand following my fingers down, each free of rope. My back to the door I put my hand on his chest spread my right out. I swallow what seems gallons of spit before I wrap the rope around his throat carefully putting a large knot against his Adam's apple. I kneel putting a leg on his chest before testing my weight to bring my leg off the floor it is then when his eyes come open. The rope still tied around his neck he pushes me down to the floor I grab the ends wrapping them around his neck using his weight to bring him to the floor. Face to face I watch his eyes whiten as he goes limp on top of me. The rope slackens in my hands and I smile at his blank face before cutting the rope and turning him over his breath a wet cough as he slams my head into the door. The door right there. The one I slipped my hand around and turned caressing the knob listening for him. If he's not with me then where would he be but dead? His cold flesh still laid out on a corner's table perhaps here? I turn the knob into a dark hallway seeing the elevator I look for the stairs with my hand and descend hitting the bottom I return up a flight and pop the door. It's bright but there is no one in sight and it's quiet. A cart with scrubs sits next to an open closet. I pull in the cart and close the door changing into pale green scrubs. Out in the hallway I hear foot steps steady following the corridor and passing the closet. I stand there smelling the detergent and soft musk. The door flies open and I fold up the gown I was wearing as the nurse asks me how I got in the linen closet, she steps back and offers me a hand I take it letting her lead me down the hallway and into a room with a pale yellow blanket and sheets. "I'm not sure which one you are here but this bed is free and someone will figure it out in the morning.

Now please stay in bed I'm new here and you shouldn't get me in trouble, I'd like to stay." With that she checks both my wrists and even ankles then tucking me in she smoothes the blinds before closing the door behind her I watch her shadow pause before receding under the door. I'm tired and much warmer in this bed. My eye lids close and I drift off.

He's shaking my shoulder I slap him barely denting his cheek but he digs his fingers in and drags me off the bed. The sheet beneath me as he uses it to drag me through the room until I slide off to stand in the doorway, he knocks me down, I land face up his knees on my shoulders. Staring at me his lips quivers then sighing he slips his knees onto the floor resting his weight on my chest. My lungs whimper my body cowers it's the ceiling behind him as his face comes closer to mine I suck air. I hear my breath as he slaps me a few times to fill each lung. I find a faint smell of cologne rolls my stomach doubled over I am beside the yellow bed huffing holding my nose. The quiet holds as I watch the light under the door steady a line separating night from day. At the door my hands flat on the metal, I push the lever and into the hallway I step barefoot the light slap faster as I run to the shadows. The door's push bar gives the air is sweet and spring engulfs me in blooming weeds of a split cracked up parking lot.

I want to be what you live for it is me and only me for you that should I leave you. You would destroy yourself and anything for me. Pledge it all to me. It's all or nothing even my breath tells you. I need to make that leap, to give myself. I have found nothing worthy of the organ not even myself. My heart it's far too heavy to carry. I love the thrill of my flesh. The important lumps, the ones in the palms of his hands. As I can't trust my mouth, can't trust these hands as they slip up my throat I drop to my knees bend over slipping my hands around my calves. I can hear crickets. The parking lot recedes into a field of grey. Swallowed up as if the building glowed. I stand and turn to follow a wall smelling gravel. Then keep walking one pace until the building falls behind. The side of the building is darkness confirming that the building is not glowing it disappears in one turn. At the edge of the shadow I stand letting my eyes adjust. Where ever I'm going maybe a long walk. I'm still wearing the scrubs the top is damp but I'm shivering unable to take one step into darkness. I take a deep breath and sit down in the shadow facing more darkness. I lay down to rest sweating, shaking convulsing, unable to stand I think about him.

On the cold metal drawer I spread out
my shoulders to the concrete lay out palms
down sighing would they rest his head with the
missing right eye up or settle his skull evenly.
Would they see the bite marks or had they
healed? He tasted tanned leather on his
shoulders.   The inside curve of his thighs
where pale blue and red until he threaded them.
I don't trust these thoughts anymore.   I can't
stop my heart it's a train wreck but it's rolling
right through me as I slam his chest under my
thighs. I'm weightless as he flips me on my
back I stare at his blue, blue eyes I feel him
panting. I hear the birds chirping slipping
sugar into the girth of their chirps. I am drawn
up into Doll's arms I turn my head as Birdie is
keeping time as she nods to me. Their mouths
singing about panic. I feel their wrists fingers
over my forearms I hear the door pop blinded
by white I close my eyes.

It calls to me. Sweet yes I hear his
voice. I hear him calling my name. It feels
heavy and I reach up for him. My hand it's
trembling as he ties my hands behind my back
kneeling on the wood my face I smell bleach. I
smell him. I hear the cracks as he shifts his
weight with each stroke the belt ripples my skin
quivering my cheek slipping down a plank. It's
his thumb pinching my ear as I slide back into
his groin. I am rage and darkness. Still I can

not cry out, open my eyes see him as he runs
his fingers over my ridged thighs. Watch as he
licks a slow steady line from each side. He
stops to watch me watch him and then snarling
at me kneeling over me it's the turn of his wrist
as I rock with his strokes. He closes his left eye
and squints at me. I close my right I can hear
the throb of the belt in the distance. I can feel
my body tremble as Doll strokes my hair.
When I turn my head she fusses over the pillow
fluffing it. Her mouth puckered trying not to
move. It's the sound of soft leather straps and I
relax thinking about what my life has become.
A whimpering strike of thunder tastes like
metal but I can't moisten my mouth. I long to
hear his voice again. My hands are on my
thighs under the blankets I test my nails
dragging them up my inner thighs. Dragging
along each scab he would pour scotch over my
body suck it off me, out of me. Drink me until
I was dry and crisp waiting for the wind to
carry my cascaras. All tryst up my thighs to
my forearms his mouth down my ass as he tells
me a story about the skin that belongs to him
the flesh that he needs to have at his mercy.
"you were mine alive, dead, before you had
breath. you waited for me. but you were bad
and didn't behave while you waited. How
filthy your thoughts are and impure I hope it
was fun. I hope you enjoyed life before me.

before my love saved you from the pain of your existence. " I watched his eyes as he spilled me out onto all fours freeing my hands to re anchor me to the floor. Pulling my head back resting my shoulders on his thighs he ran his hands down my backside slapping the corded muscle of my arms, thighs and buttocks. I know the sound of his pant miles beneath my pain. The ache brings the jelly to steel and loosening the rope I push off the floor to slam him into the wall knocking his breath out but leaning into him only to have his weight land on me. I feel the knife as he cuts my ropes snarling before I slip my foot free wedging his wrist to the floor. It's the rope around my neck and with his foot between my shoulders I am docile again. Smoothed out silver between his fingers. His rich coo ebbing each ounce. Would he be smiling laid out on the drawer? Possibly a glint still in his eye? The blue of my new eye it's a bold cut and I close my left. I stare up at what I wish was the stars I don't need to reach for them or even see their glow, I stroke my chest laying under him. The warmth of his spit as he wipes his face on my cheek laying his body over mine and inside me it is that throb that fire that snuffs me out. I am flooded with tears as the oxygen chills my insides. I open my eyes he's cutting potatoes at the sink I on my stool not tied but draped my limbs rock. It's night

eternal night and he's cooking, boiling water.
Lots of water, pots on all the burners, a tall grey
specked, he leans over it smiling back at me.
He turns a needle in hand strokes my shoulder
with it taps my cheek. My face in his hands he
licks my swollen lips takes the needle back
through the stitches clicking his tongue as the
threads squeak His nostrils flare and he pulls a
pair of scissors from the counter rolling the tip
over my upper lip he spreads his fingers over
my jaw palming my chin. I quiver as the snips
split his pauses as he hums. With forceps the
bits of thread are tugged out of my lips after he
inspects each one it is his thumb he uses to
spread out my lips and explore my mouth.

      I watch the kitchen curtain dance over
the small window I see a bird. It's blue head
brighter than the light of the kitchen he bobs
slamming his beak into the window sash. Then
his head and slides down the pane disappearing,
the counter top holds my weight the double
sink is empty a tea towel is spread out with
needles, thread, floss, and a bottle of whiskey.
I'm resting my weight on my hips but leaning
on a cabinet door. His lips are moving I see his
breath and feel the heat of his mouth as he
cradles my face his eyes blue bright blue and he
closes his left eye. I see myself the hospital
gown dingy smells of plastic flowers. I can't
find my feet, my hands and the right eye closes

leaving me in the darkness, a soundless vacuum.

What's a girl to do? My heart it's a dangerous thing trapped in a body only I will die for. A crumpled history, what else could explain such desire? What would it matter to you? To anyone? What heart could survive what heart could lust for enraged and betray the will to live. But I haven't died. I am powerless giving everything to chance. Reason betrays us all and emotion only tortures it's not about a good heart but a strong one. I stand before his bathroom mirror caressing my freshly stitched lips he slaps my face telling me not be vain. "sure not every girl can be so loved. Lucky girl thirteen. supple, sweet and all mine always." I put my arms at my sides then on the sink edge then behind my back he watches me smiling the rope doubled in his hand. Kneeling down, the back of his head a soft fur and I place my hand on it. Grabbing my ankles he flips me over his shoulder and down the hall we go. I let my nails drag the walls. He slams me to the floor in the hallway rolls me over to tie my hands, my elbows and then over the other shoulder into the bed pushed to the wall. I feel the springs stir I feel cold then melted. My mouth waters he kneels me against his thighs to slide the belt around my throat and then lowers my head to the floor.

His lip quivers as he tightens the belt I don't look away I stare his white blue eyes and he dumps the belt strips it from my neck and pets my face then slaps me as I breath again. I suck up the fresh bloody whiskey soaked stitches, my nerves are slippery pulses he lays me on the bed untying me to drape my arms over my chest carefully to place the fingers of each hand. He pets my face again and then standing up he takes off his pants. I hold my breath as he slides me over in the bed then when he turns his back I push him to the floor slamming his head only once before grabbing his belt off the floor. His neck is thicker than mine and he smiles when I tighten the belt. I pull my knees under myself leaning back to use his chest for leverage. His face goes white and I loosen the belt grab his cheeks before slapping him. I get in 4 hard lefts before his mouth comes open coughing tossing me to the floor. On his hands and knees he vomits on the floor. Still white the bluest hue, corpse like a color he certainly must now be as his skin grows reptilian on the undertaker's slab.

I put my right hand under my left breast it's healing the scabs smoothed over ripples. I'm stroking my ribs counting them. Their sturdy and I trail down sitting up in the narrow bed as I count my toes. My hands shake I feel this faint vibration as if I was radiating. I let out a long sigh and then run my fingers over my lips. All my teeth, all my bones and where could I be now. I hear footsteps and lay down in the bed pulling the blanket up over my hands. It's warm without smell the building seems to swallow sound. I drift off.

It's birds muffled through the glass I smell blood I turn my head opening my eyes to the blank wall then turn onto my side staring at the closed door he's beside me sleeping soundly in the faint morning. I lay on my back resting my arm on the curve of his ass. My hand fingers spread over the slope, after a few minutes he rolls over slipping the rope over my hands one by one securing them to the frame of the bed. He sits straddling me traces down lingering to probe each rib. Leaving the room the birds soft then silent as he returns with a tray. My mouth waters I think of caramel burnt in my veins I twitch vibrating as my heart stutters. My stomach growls before the burst hits my veins. From slip to shine I ooze the silence is painful but there isn't anything to fill it. My overripe heart engorges itself swells pushing each soft stroke away. It's never anything like sadness. I can't shed a tear over my selfish whims. I can't woo darkness when I radiate my own eerie glow. I'm running up the steep drop of the ravine it's rocky and the rim is grass sticking to my knees. I had to sink my hands into the spongy grass to stand and look over my shoulder. I shiver the fall wind picks up dry leaves as I trudge into the trees. Under the first tree I pause listening looking at the lit up bridge where the lights only reveal the concrete. He's there standing on the bridge in only his jeans barefoot and each step faster as he comes toward me. There's no reason to run I smile watching him fling me to grass. I disappear find the blades soft as I fall onto my back facing up his face over me. I reach for him. He stands there it begins to rain the drops harder churning the sky. I'm covered in his sweat laying over me as the eruptions smell heavy upon my skin.

My hands and feet are numb, my loins throb I'm racing to find anything to quail the sound of my icy heart. My breath is hot and I hold my lips closed scared of the fire snaking out. Bubbles ripple my throat vibrating my ribs. I am sore sagging skin on veins hanging through the bones. I dig at the tears trying to unearth the source of heat. Making a way for it to escape my trembling jelly. I hear my heart calling me back to stroke the glass with my ear. It says what is life with out love? Without passion? With out Death, what is life? We all know how it ends Death. Dirt, debris, dust not one thing has survived time. Time is the grim reaper's best torture. It may be true that the strong survive but time is never beaten only advanced on.

I remember the people in the supermarket I never thought of them before or how they disgusted me. Their loud rude children, their unwashed sections hanging out as they scratch mouth open gazing over the shiny surfaces of greed. It horrified me to see anyone chose to live with such self loathing and ignorance. He smelled different. I can close my eyes and smell Him drifting in the room. How would I comfort a heart driven to implode? Who could be trusted to not steal my time away to rob me of the fight in my limbs? To try and shorten the thrill, I'm unable to lay my flesh down and surrender. It is only be sheer and slim chance I meet Him. I would have waited a life time wasted as many days until I met Him. He cried in my arms, finished sucking a fresh breath the back of his hand stroking my limp chest I heard his tears I pulled in a cold breath. I could not deny Him even as he took everything from me. I hear the plastic feel it stroke my ear as I crinkle it rolling my stiff hip and open my eyes. He's crouched over me his grey eyes wet red rimmed he holds my face the warmth of his fingers. My lips I can't not smile, I can't feel anything but the heat of his

skin and he strokes my arms arranges me
before folding the sheeting to cover my face.

In this silence I am startled by the
thought of death. Where is his love? Here in
the frosted plastic? My heart sizzles then
throbs open and inside I am wet with its
explosion. I can feel hot tears warming my
face. I can feel the weight of my flesh and the
pinch of the rope over my chest. I pull up my
hands slipping a digit over my chin and into my
mouth. Biting it I push the rope loose and hear
the hiss of refrigerated air as I turn on my side
aware of the metal shelf I lay on. I follow the
turn of the wrapping finding the corner with my
fingers push through my left hand trembling. I
palm a cold concrete slab dusty it sticks to my
fingers and I slip my hand under the plastic to
examine the powdery ice. My breath melts it.
If I lay here, how long could I lay here? I listen
to my heart ripping out of my chest shaking the
creased plastic. Now…now it says what good
is love now? I put my foot out the side and
letting the plastic fall with me land on the floor
it's only a couple feet but every bone felt
gravity. On my back I open my eyes looking
up seeing the shelves lining the room. Rolling
over I stand stare at the floor as I rise up to my
full height. It's narrow and my shoulders brush
the icy metal and then rest on a flap of stiff
plastic. I stare at my feet the gurgle of my

stomach drowning out the compressor.
Turning my head I can see her laid out on her
back, hands over her breasts her long blonde
hair her pouty red lips. The pert rise of each
nipple I put my hand over her face stroke it
through the fold. Her head is turned facing me,
I unfold a small section over her chest and slip
my warm hand under her left breast finding it
smooth, then the right smiling over the un
blemished skin. I fold her up careful to not
disturb her skin. Milky her eyes are closed she
could be a fairy tale. I take a deep cold breath
rub my hands as I lean forward to shove open
the door. it gives and gingerly I step onto the
wood floor letting the weight of the door close
behind me. I stand there an eternity. I think
about his eyes. I crouch resting my back on the
closed door. Draw up my knees to my chest as
I hear him singing down the hallway. A lover
is pleading but I swell with each note. Striding
down the hallway I pause watching him head
thrown back his hands over his heart. The
crack of a guitar and he turns seeing me he
holds out his hands. I slap him as he reaches
for the knife on the counter. I slam my body
into him taking him to the floor where I pin him
face down pummel his shoulders before he flips
me into the cupboard door. I sink my teeth into
his shoulder and he pulls at my hips his voice
quivering as he licks me down my face. It's

cinnamon, cigarettes and sweat his sweet taste blood on my tongue as he draws me up into his arms using his belt he restrains my hands over my head and using the flat of the knife slaps my ass eyeing me his pupils opals as he lays the knife on the floor to undo his pants his scar trembles as he growls at me. he pushes his thumb under my jaw I smile letting my lips fall open he licks my face before he fucks me grunting biting my throat. Over his head I see the stain of the little bird's blood smeared on the glass. But there's another bird chirping helplessly head cocked to and fro. He switches back and forth as the warmth runs out my ears. It grows dark but I can taste his blood. I can feel him inside me pounding our hearts to the floor. His breath runs out and he turns me over his knee slipping the belt off my hands to secure my feet. On the counter he rests me laying my head on the wet wooden board. He stands over me stroking my hair closing his right eye he tells me I ruin everything. His lips smile and I try to decide if the knife is on the floor. I close my left eye. My hands are free and pushing off the counter I roll up onto my knees the cutting board slides easily off the side and I slap his face with it pushing him to the floor the board breaks over his chest when we land. Silence as I undo my feet and lean over his body his right eye stares at me I pause hanging until a rap on the window startles him blinking he slips his tongue over his bloody teeth spitting on me and licking my face, I smell a sweet sickness from his mouth. Holding me chest throbbing to mine he bites my neck scratches down the shoulder and I can see the knife under the cabinet door. The licks of the belt make me gasp he finds a rhythm stopping to squeeze my cheek I feel the tip ripple stick take the very quiver from my lips into each slow soft sound. My heart had such a throb still oozing combusted inside me. I coughed wondering if my lungs could handle heavy air.

Wondering when will I find nirvana again. I can take my thoughts away, steal time without skin but peace never lingers. Still is broken by every reverberation of life around me. The hum of this society screaming selfish, loathing their own wills as they murder the evolution that gave them the ability to wish it away. In the bath tub he keeps me in his lap washing the smears of his blood off my face off his chest. I no longer have hair as he pours water over my face rinsing behind my ears. The water slopes over the side I lean forward resting on the edge as he slides behind me pouring water over my ass the stings of the soap. The water ripples as I quiver pressed against him wet in the tub the bathroom door stands open the heat of this night is intense. There are bags of ice on the floor and he dumps one down my back before sitting me in the tub facing him. After each bag of ice I watch his scar tighten his lip. Then his hands under the ice up inside me where the dull ache persists. He pulls me onto his lap bracing me on the edge of the tub. I can hear his breath over my heart. I turn my head seeing my face in the mirror. My pale blue skin the bruises down my neck I close my right eye turning toward him as he begins to cry out. More a murmur than words then his teeth chattering as he wraps his arms around me to lay with me. My heart falls faint hissing in the ice, his mouth has fallen open and I shove my fingers in there; but his weight it's on my arm. I lay there listening to ice melting.

I wondered if this would kill him as his heart seemed sluggish with mine. I began to kick shifting the ice and rolling him further into the tub I, now able to pull myself over the edge, tumble onto the floor. The floor was covered in empty wet ice bags they slipped as I hoisted myself up to stand running my fingers down his wrist looking for a pulse unable to stop shaking long enough. I put my cold hands in my mouth and turned towards the mirror then when my leg gave way I braced myself to stand both hands on the dry porcelain. Still quiet the hot air steamed as I popped the window pane unable to open it. He coughed still twitching in the melting ice. Then when silence returned I sat on the toilet looking down the hallway. My convulsions over took me and I landed on the floor where he found me after he rose from the tub dripping ice over me as he gathered me up to fling me into the tub. Leaving the room he shuts the door. There's that taste that electric melted crap in my mouth film and I'm spitting out imaginary cotton balls onto the floor at his feet. I can smell the bleach on the stark white tile. See my hands spread out in front of me feel the wet leather eat the corners of these damp day mares. The echo it's my heart beat cracking dodging the lightning ripping my chest snaking from the floor up into my limbs. I am all rain, draining out my pores melting the white tile with the heat flowing from my skin. He's licking my face telling me how lucky, how lucky we are.

I'm the lucky one. It dawns on me. laying face up on the white tile. I smile take a deep sigh resting in his arms the electric blue of his eyes. I feel the breeze rifling blades of glass whipping my naked skin I look up into the clouds. The raspy darkness swallows me sweat drips down my face I open my mouth feel the wind hollow my lips. I can say nothing for myself I lingered in every look. I sunk my teeth into his shoulders, I scratched and cam with him all gash. Our breathless nights any one of them could have been my last and this night it's no different. There is no longer him. I try to see his face in the puffy clouds arc into the wind to find him calling me. But it's empty, I am all alone in this field. I hold my hands up but I worry some one will find me and take me from these thoughts. What is it the world thinks about? Those daily occurrences rapid fire amusements the truly mounds of preoccupation.

I have all I need inside my skin. I put my hands over my face close my eyes but I can't see his face I see my face over the hospital sink. I see that white blue eye rolling up to greet me. I smile it's spectacular and distracting the iris exploded out, I'm a rag doll in his arms he bathes me taking all my hair off. I run my hands over his head and he shaves all of it off and returns to the tub. The water is warm we fit, me in his lap my feet over the edge. He traces the scabs and fresh scars kissing them. some scabs he tears at with his teeth. I spit bath water at him first a drop then a stream until he puts my face in the water. Holds me down my hands are free and I brace them using his thighs, digging my short cut nails in. The water is pink around my fingers he pulls my head up and slaps me, by the throat he slips me head first over the tub edge. I wrap my legs around his chest take him with me if possible but as I feel my shoulders glide down the tub inside the water rises and I watch his face. His eyes grey as he jerks off drowning me but he isn't hard. His dick flops in his hands a few times and then he pull the plug on the drain letting the water tease me until my lips feel the air.   We sit there in the tub while listening to it drain. He dries me off takes me to the kitchen and injects me with a syringe before tying me onto the stool. I'm watching him lay out a needle, thread and petroleum jelly but I'm cold. I feel wet, the stool is cold and runs up into my nose. Massaging my lips he makes faces at me rubbing salve across the cracks of my lower lip. When I bare my teeth he puts the tip of his fingers spreading the upper lips out coating it. The taste is greasy, my mouth drools unable to wash it away. He wipes my teeth with a washcloth checking my tongue before tugging my lips closed face to face pupil to pupil. I'm all smile as he returns the smile then bares his canines back handing me. I spit blood on the floor and return upright on the stool. I keep my lips over my teeth. Ignoring me he turns and begins to hum. It sounds like doubt he steals glances at me as I melt on my stool. It feels heavy every inch of my skin. My lips stick to my teeth, my mouth is cotton. He goes on his hands chopping potatoes the smell of boiling water. It's hot I'm drowning in my sweat. I'm slippery on the kitchen floor the knife reflecting the window.

The window still stained but on the inside I lean out to run my fingers over the knife hear him slap me off the stool. I hear a boy calling me over the rush of a highway headlights over the grass. I see the sky turn grey his face staring down at blinded by the rising sun over his shoulder. He's calling me it's loud and clear. He's rolling the crumpled plastic over me again this time tying me in place with zip ties. I feel my face smile, am I dead? I want to lift my hand to check I want to touch him. His cheek is cold and after his face disappears I close my eyes heavy with frost. I am up running down the side of the river barefoot, naked and mud in my hair these's not a person in sight and the fade of the highway blends into crickets. I stop stand still huffing coughing before flinging myself down to vomit rub dirt in my teeth to kill the taste of the acid erupting from my lips. Bent over on all fours I take a clean breath reaching out to put my hand in the river. Lazy nearly still cold but warm as I splash my face. I'm on the freezer's concrete floor pulling my hands around to my front numb brushing the crust off the fresh blood around my wrists. I stand using the metal leg

of the shelves and feel the wall until the circle
knob is giving way and I lean letting myself fall
into the hallway. I lay there pulling my legs
through before being able to swing free. I hear
the birds. No settled dust I smell bleach. Using
the closed door I get to my knees. Shuffle
down the hallway to my open door where he
lays sleeping draped over the bed. There's
glass under the edge of the bed he continues to
lay there his breath even I watch him as the
plastic around my ankles begins to give I work
my feet free and crouch stepping close to the
bed. I split the last tie when he rolled over eyes
closed lower lip slacked. I waited suddenly
unsure. His eyes didn't open but he raises his
nostrils as I cover my mouth with my hands my
own breath could betray me, but my heart skips
as he settles into an even sigh. Smelling
whiskey I take the rope from the corner post
and slip the knots out before coiling it around
his throat and then to the bed's upper corner
and keeping the extra slack with me as I trail
myself out of the room tying the end to the door
taunt rising from underneath the bed I slam the
door leaning my back on the door to face him
as his hands go to his neck. He gasps for air
reaching to slack the rope as I wind a leg
around it before pulling it toward me. His
shoulder snaps into the wall. Turning he
pounds the wall then flattens his hands out

unable to breath. Keeping the rope snaked on my arm I follow it back the bed where He lays, ready should he be playing possum. My twitching fingers trail up the curve of his shoulder and before I feel his lungs exhale he is rolling back shoving me to the floor taking the bed over until it rests on us. Pushing the mattress off I scramble to stand finding him using the loop I put around his head to bind my feet then flipping the bed he finishes hog tying me. Wipes his mouth, coughs then shoves the bed frame back he turns smiling at me then flops the mattress into pace he leaves the room slapping me across the thighs as he steps over me. The door stands wide open but I can only see the wood floor. Hear his steps down the hallway as he opens the freezer door then slams it.

I'm not ready to die. Can my heart fathom a life misspent? I think about the taste of the blood in my mouth, the throb of my heart against the floor I relax the rope takes the weight of my limbs. My right cheek pressed into a board as the footfalls of his return chatter my teeth. He sits down beside me on the floor his elbows resting on his knees takes a drag off a cigarette taps the floor with his foot as he rocks slightly. Strokes my face pushes my head to rest my left cheek turning away from him. his left hand slips under my left breast

then his right lifting me up and rolling me onto
the bed still face down. His exhale in my ear
the smoke curls over my lobe. I hope for a
pinch. The sweetness filling my mouth but his
probing fingers fill my empty cavity I push my
chest up the wall but the bed gives as he digs
his thumbs into the hollow of my hips
mounting me. The dry squeak shivers my spine
and goose bumps litter my surface. I open my
mouth let my teeth rub the wall. Inside me
each organ melts even his as he curses falling
out of my cavity. My shoulders hit the floor
and the wetness of the belt is my blood. It licks
me I can hear his heaving huff feel the air
ripple as he drops the belt stepping over me to
rub his groin over my bloody thigh. Then
crouching down he sinks his teeth into my ass,
licks the wet slosh down my inner thigh.
Untying me before restraining me properly to
the wooden chair he leaves the room door open
and down the hallway he steps lightly I lose his
footfalls in the birds chirping. I can barely
keep my head up and I lounge on my right
shoulder drooling blood down my tit. I close
my eyes. I don't want to see him, smell him, or
taste him but there's no escape. A quiver fills
my heart rippling the skin is this love? Unable
to leave unable to stay.

Birdie strokes my face the wash clothe
warm white as I open my eyes she trills leaning

in to kiss my cheek. Her smile wet lipstick bright catching the light her bottom lip tremble belting out a sad ballad. The words mean little her face soft brushing my hair fussing over the nearly healed rips, tears on my face. I put my fingers over her breast looking for a rhythm. Cup the slope inching into her collar, blocking my hand she stands clears her throat. I lay there I can smell her perfume in the air above I close my eyes as if drifts over my face. In the quiet I hear birds spread out clinks on the frosted glass. His breath on my face syrupy turning the dew to mist, He's laying on me in the grass and the stars level the bleakness of the slow slap of my heart in my throat. I think about space spans of time traveled searching for similarity. Gravity pulling the weight of my heart into the earth. Always wreckage beyond salvage when colliding with the speed of progress given the calculations of each mass towards it's own destruction. If we are all damaged then why is it we believe it can be cured? Find the root of what ails a human. Why throw life out of each equation? Why allow time to be invisible? He's listening to my heart orbiting him. He's the gravity pulling me back. Without him would I float errantly out? What else is beyond my knowledge? What other life could I lead? These four walls feel the same no matter which room they belong to. A caged animal I twitch the wind flips leaves over the window I hear crickets filling up my name. turn my head put a hand over each ear what is it to be called sent running at the whim of the night? All my power and grace rolling up on the wood grain shivering as the moon looms through the frost. He's howling behind me putting my face on the glass resting my hands on the panes, letting me see out. Letting me feel the moon stare as he pounds my flesh. I ball up my fists fling each one into the glass thud bouncing as I try again he laughs pinning them down to cup my ass leaning over into my ear his freight train pant wearing himself thin. I don't hear birds. There are no insects as his teeth nip at my neck. There are no flowery words here. No bright hopeful future. It's my pulse base lining as he shuts the sounds of life from me. As he steams squawking the fury of futile desire. Insatiable his thirst the demand to be. I am all but quelled folded at his feet my breath a cloud dripping from my mouth. I find myself chest out up on my knees deep in the grass. Arms filled with stars the wind roaring through my pores. I hear him calling my name. Calling each syllable then shouting. The rain hisses down my face. My tears fill the empty drops rolling down my chest I run my hands over my mouth. Over my lips take a breath through my wet digits. The rain is cold I burn yearn to hear him as thunder slaps lighting near the river. My thighs twitch I stroke the scars I search through the cotton blankets for my bare skin. I open my eyes seeing Doll smoothing out the fall of my dark hair over my right shoulder. She swoons her breast filled with a murmuring note. Stroking my face her lips their red paint perfect I put my hand over hers she rests it there on my cheek. I take two of her fingers in my mouth turning slightly raising up from the pillow. Her eyes as she looks away but does not take her hand.

My chest steams my loins eating away at my rotting flesh. A slow throb an earthquake centering in my hips. Buckling my knees I push against gravity my head is heavy the air keeps getting sucked from me. I won't stop struggling I can't let myself. Each hand a fist as I punch the sky. I grab at the surface of my chest running my hands up trying to locate the pressure. Trying to gain advantage over my limbs. The floor is concrete a sheet of ice my flesh feels numb. I can't taste or feel my lips but fingers slide over a stitch as I open my eyes. Alone in the freezer, never really alone in his freezer. I can hear them birds screaming high pitched fighting over morsels to survive. I put my hands over my ears knowing they can't see me half buried in the mud of the river. The flap of their wings vultures sniffing out a rotten body. Bloodhounds in the distance. A full moon I roll over run a finger under my left breast buttery smooth as the water rises over me. opening my mouth mud pours down my throat. Maybe no one is searching for me. Maybe I am dead a corpse in a river, wrapped from frost, but there's a well of mire invading my brain.

I wake up on the floor where he tossed me out of the bed. Sun light drifts through the settling dust, he sits on the bed his feet on my chest. Leaning forward thumps his thumb on my sternum. I hear the crack of ice as my heart shakes loosening the refrigerator, I wait for speed up that slips loose the housing. The crash, I listen for the crash and a take a big breath. It's still me and I'm mostly here. The void of flesh I am carving out has only made me lighter, free. Am I my flesh, or blood, or bone? Am I all of it? This piece I gave away, this I prayed would rot off first. I'm looking in the mirror at the blue eye I lean forward into my reflection. I can't hear anything.

My ear drums feel sucked in and letting out my breath to fill each lunge hot burning the frost out. His chest feels soft he lays his head on my thigh as stroke his hair he's smiling but my fingers are around his throat. It's not a responsive smile as pace my own heart beat through my thighs I stand up. Roll him over face up and slapping him repeatedly. Smiling down at him the pale wash of color pops in his face his irises tightening before his nostril flares. I put my knees into his shoulder pits using my angular frame. Resting on his chest I stare at him he takes slow measured breaths and coughs his eyes a murky blue as he stares back. He puts his hands up my thighs unseats me and tosses me into the open doorway I stand up not clearing the door before I feel his hand around my ankle. Gravity wins and I land on the floor. His chuckling as he tugs me down the wood, my free hands I slap at him then lean down catching his face. A hard plop as he pulls the belt out of his pants. It's wet and after the first lick I let out my sigh. Quivered no longer hearing his breath but my own heart. I turn wrapping the belt around one hand pulling him to the floor my feet on his knees. My face wet on the wood as he puts the belt around my elbows bringing them together behind my back. The skin of my chest burns, up and onto the plain wooden chair he sits me tying my ankles to one leg. He pours booze down my front and I can feel the raw flesh under my left breast. If my heart were to escape this would be how it fled me. He tells me how I belong to him and there isn't anything real but he and I, thirteen, his lucky girl. He believes in love but forgives me for being any other man's whore before

him. Before I knew him. Still I will be
punished after all I am thirteen. why did I wait
so long? Didn't my heart know how to find
him? Could I not remain pure? Before I knew
him my loins should have not twitched. It
should have been his gaze that made me burn.
"you are my girl, can't be without me." He
sterilizes the needles then turns smiling. "tell
me you love me. tell me you long to be with me
forever even in death." I spread my lips as I
feel myself turn the corners up the words are
lost in his blue eyes. I bite my upper lip as he
kisses me licking my teeth wetting them.
Leaning back the needle slips through my
bottom lip as he licks my shoulder. the tip
resting in the fresh scab before following
through the top lip. He licks my shoulder
biting it. Drawing back to slap me to tighten the
first stitch. I smile at him smiling at me I feel
gooey, gobs of dripping saliva down my chin.
Sucking on my lips he then takes a swig of
whiskey before spitting it over my mouth. I
rest my chin in his left palm. The whiskey
beads on his lips he wipes it away with the back
of his right hand clutching the needle and
thread. Plotting the next stitch his pupils widen
out he clears his throat returning to my gaze
once he places the needle. He smiles again as it
passes through both lips back handing me then
wrapping his hand around my neck. He pulls

me closer licks the running blood. Moans in my ear before turning my head to pin the next hole. Then at my ear he holds his breath slamming the tip through both lips but pausing to let out his breath. He slaps me a few times the chair dances a slow tango. Then sliding the chair to the edge of the bed he tugs the needle free and tightens the stitch with his teeth, licking my throbbing mouth. My eyes well up and it's birds screeching, slamming their wings into the current. I gasp slowly letting my body throb. Whistling leaves along the ground gravel I'm on my knees his teeth rubbing the new stitches. "If you won't speak for me then you will never speak to anyone again." He lights the end of the thread then spits licking out the burn. Admiring his work he shifts my head side to side in his palms smiling the curl of his fingers down my throat. His eyes well up he snarls then lets me slip to the floor down his leg putting my face toward the door. I can see it's open I can see as he lays his face next to mine his blue eyes white hot and I pull my lips tight he stands walks out the door leaves it open his feet down the hall. I hurt as my knees are dug into the floor I push back finding my ankles to draw up my head. Silence, not sweet but caustic I leave my face on the floor and survey the door looking for shadows. Listening to the birds. The birds rippling in I don't hear him but I see him walk into the room shut the door and step over me. He fucks me drawing up my back against his chest chewing on my ear. His panting a hard puff in my ear, He climaxes losing balance landing on me on the floor. He stands up puts me on the bed chest thrust forward licks his brand.

It's so quiet but I must not open my eyes. I hear my heart roll out against my breath. Holding it I wet my lips moist, cold as I cough. I lean forward unable to stop convulsing pull up my knees to my chest feel the cotton sheets tug tighten and sitting up put my hands over my mouth. It's dark but the walls glow grey the wind fumbles by the glass. It's only me I throw back the sheets flex my toes. Running my fingers over my face and down my neck I draw up my chest stopping on the healed ridges. I let out my breath and slip over the side to creep naked to the door. I peer through the crack unable to see down the hallway. I sit against the closed door listening I can smell Doll's lotion on my hands, my arms and licking a finger taste it too. Grimacing I spit a hard cough looking about the glowing walls. There are no birds, no sounds of life as I slide up the door to stand. I press my front to the door leaning my weight onto my toes. I think about his chest as I stroke the door, his fur, and the soft hair of his thighs. I close my eyes. I want to hear him. hear him call my name. hear him sing the doubt of my love. How he told me I wouldn't be alone ever again. He didn't know the future but we will always be together. He would tie me in the bed secure me before bringing out the needle. He needed time to think he said. He smiled getting under the sheet with me.

He was my world, pain, joy, and every breath I took my body it craved his attention. Sickness wells up into my mouth and I crash to the floor on all fours. Punching my fists into the door I see the door come towards me and feel the pop in my forehead. I am awash my quivering thighs throb he's pouring vodka over my back and I stand knocking the bottle from his hand. He stands there face to face with me my lips wet he slaps me twice then scooping me over his shoulder we stomp into the kitchen where he lands me on the floor taking the frying pan off the stove to break the handle off on my hip. I kick him and grip his legs flipping him down onto me. His breathing is heavy as he pins my shoulders with his thighs, spits in my face and I use my feet to slam his head into the cabinet. He grabs the counter and slides us away from the walls. Bringing his hands to under my rib cage he uses his weight to pin me. His breath evens out he clears his throat. Stands up steps over me to open the freezer and taking out a bag of ice he slams it onto my face. The plastic is dry and sticks to my face he slaps the ice bag shifting it off my head before picking it up and doing it again. The ice bag pops finally spilling ice over the floor around me. He drags the bag around knocking out the ice then tossing the bag in the sink. Licking my face he rubs the ice over my body then licks my lips before piling ice over them, the stitches feel stiff. I watch him unable to move I feel my hot breath and staggering heart beat. I hear sirens blowing in the distance watch hum turn his head listening still until the siren fades out, he, cocked to the side, looks out of his eye at me. I lay there staring up at him. The ice is all but melted pooling under me. still cold as he turns me over and I hear his foot falls. The floor is grey with specks of black. A tile not a real tile but rolled out in vinyl. It's dim soft as twilight but unable to move I can't hear anything. Can't feel my lips. I turn my head then stand crouched on my heels I rise up leaning on the counter to steady. I turn facing the rest of the kitchen. I collapse when I hear a door slam. His bare feet stand in the doorway to the kitchen he taps one foot then crosses to me flipping me over taking my shoulder into the floor. His eyes moon over me twin globes white built as he sweeps down to collect my limp body. I roll over his shoulder my knuckles gracing his sagging back pockets. String muscle I twitch as he scratches the wall leading down that hall using his weight to let me feel his footsteps. I can't hear a breath my own or his and there is only now like a sharp pop. I see the ceiling I feel my lungs fill up and hitting bottom never thrust me up into the heavens kicking all my cells loose. I am all the molecules. I am higher than any star in his universe. I am beyond his flesh, his desire of my tortured soul. As if the need to keep me would grant my favor. I haven't the desire to stay even in my present breath I can't fight the need to let each limb lead with out any thought. Without knowing a consequence my hand flies out I slap his face. I rise up and backhand him pushing him to land in the door jam. I slap him as he drags himself up the open door I wrap a hand around his throat smiling I turn to push his chest down climbing him to place my hands around his neck. He pushes back turning to crawl a foot before I grasp his ankle. It's his toes on my jaw and the wall right after but I smile and roll over hearing him open a drawer in the living room. Each tap swiftly down the hallway I roll over using my hands to pull my body under me and stand to face the gun in his hand. He lets out his breath his lower lip quivers.

"I loved you. But your dead to me now I know what kind of a women you are sucking out hearts. I can't kill you enough. " he trembles the gun clicking in his hand gulping as he turns the gun onto his chest the tip smacking his pale sweat. "you could not survive alone. " he puts the gun and his free hand in the air turns each palm out letting the gun rest on a finger. "without me you would die. I am the only one who can take care of you. Who else is going play these games with you. You are sick and twisted." He shakes his hands huffing once " no sane person would love you. But every one you favor with your gaze will become mad. You have driven me mad I dreamed of you as a little boy. I have been waiting for you." I slapped him he points the gun to my chest and I backhand him letting my hand hit the wall. I put my palm flat on the wall as he spits blood on my feet. " you sick bitch I tell you how I love you and you treat me to silence." He's rubbing the blood off his mouth and wiping it on my face my shoulder over my sewn lips. He put his hand over my mouth smirking before laying me out on the floor. He leans over to whisper in my ear." Such an unlucky girl to be lucky I love her."

Is love so much glorious because of the pain? Will I not now despair? Without his torture, without his heart pounding at my hip, what other breath would be the gravity of the universe? I was mistaken to allow myself to orbit but I fell as I always do into planetary gravity. I will strip away the weight of existence to float out to return to the night. The sky spread stars over a velvet drape cling by drifting particles. There was never a now but an everything. tomorrow yesterday and now I want to fill up my lungs steady my feet to drift into the heavens. To set myself into a world free of such fears. The love that sets you free may also be your death. The freezer hisses I am on the floor concrete as his voice feels like cockroaches rattling I look up beyond his face see a sky mist filled rolling smoke but his face interrupts. His mouth open and lower lips directing his cheek flinching, his hands big circles and then he pauses kneeling down beside me. my face in his hands he lays onto my chest over me on the floor. A rolling thud resonates in my chest I can taste my blood and I feel the floor wet under me his face wet on me. Sweet sad boy kissing my breasts sinking his teeth into my upper arm. His face feels soft as I stare at the ceiling unsure of any thing other than his soft rasping breath. I can't see him smell him or even hear his voice but draped over me I am the gravity drawing him in. His heart melts into mine a ragged fire claiming every lover's touch.   He bathes me in kerosene but can not keep from absorbing the lethal fumes then igniting himself he figures to destroy us both. To burn our desire out.

Laying on the floor beneath him I sink into a thick mud feel the water sweep over me and I open my mouth filled with the river. Filled with thick chalk I roll over and push the weight off me see my air rise over me I look up. There's nothing there no stars, no fog but unreachable. I push the blanket of mud trying to tear every morsel off. I lift my arms drawing out my fingers to cup my hands. To stroke towards the darkness to reach each finger out and pull the darkness into my chest. I can hear thunder hear his hand strike me, know that faint odor it's putrid gasp as my belly empties.

I lean over the bed rail puking shaking sweaty the beep a steady call making me rise into a squat to roll the last churn onto the floor clear of the bed. I hear the door the swing inwards as it bangs into the bathroom door. feel my face and forehead go into the rail but then finding the floor meets me there. Where he slaps me and my eyes focus on his face, he's got my arms draped over the back of the wooden chair thrust head rolled this way and that a cracked belt he broke on my thighs keeping time. Keeping a swift flow he switches hands then licks my face straddling me. tugs on my ears spits on my lips puts the belt around one of my forearms he stands the needle pick stings. I shiver my mouth concrete pillars. He straddles me wearing his jeans inspecting my pupils tugging on my hair undoing his pants stroking his brand cooing at me. "what a good girl" he says leaving hard g's then   huffing whining that he's not getting hard for me I shall be punished. If I would understand his point of view, he taps the scalpel on the kitchen counter. Runs the tip over my nipple before dropping it on the counter he clears his throat. "Do you think you are worth all the trouble you have caused me? do you think I like the sick games you play with me?" his lip quivers then sighing he smiles. " Do you know how lucky you are to be with me? "

I can't move I can't even drool I see him standing there at the counter but one or two steps and he could be anywhere. He steps towards me his hands over my face strokes my lips. "you don't have to say nothing I know how you need me." he inspects my body secures my ankles to each front leg also under my knees the rope snakes around hissing he kneels his head between my legs looking up at me. my head lulling to the side, he removes his jeans and shaves off all his body hair then turns and takes even the hair off my head. I listen to the buzz a heavy thwack as he flips the power on and off. On and then off three times then

rubbing the hair off me a few slaps and he steps
back to turn on the sink pulling a hose with his
returning hand he wets me down pulling his
palm over the back of my head before turning
to rinse himself. I watch him turn off the faucet
and dripping still he stands there. One hand
massaging it's shoulder looking into the dark
window he leans back rubbing his face.
Turning around he rests against the counter
front, admiring my soft glowing skin he rolls
his hip rubbing himself then pulling the chair
towards him he leans into my face licking those
stitches gripping the chair with his thighs he
lowers his butt into my lap he moans cupping
my breasts the words are intangible but he's
rattling on. Chewing my ear as he fills it with
mumble, then a rattle in the chair and it gives
way sending its occupants sailing to the tile.
He pulls the chair apart using the freed sections
to beat me. His voice loud ripping the words
thrusting his face into mine on the floor. I can
smell the vodka, the pungent odor fills me but
only my bones give me away rattling as the
broken chair splinters on the floor around me.
he grabs my arms, still bound behind, dragging
me down the hallway the floor feels sanded by
my skin. I hear the scraping whine hear the
door bang and feel myself lift off the floor thud
onto the bed. It doesn't seem real the colors
smudged hazy and dampened words fill my

head. Slapping my forearm he's got a needle between his teeth up close he's a cartoon smile, the gooey drop of my tendons, I know his voice but it never reaches me here. I know his touch but not under these ink and tar stains. It's my heart bursting out it's my free hands slapping him as he ties me to the bed as he takes each wrist tying it securely to one post. He breathes in one ear a huff, a pounding wave, his humanity sickens me. His spittle down my ears the panting rasp of his release. The blubbering pity "I don't mean to hurt you but I have to, I have to" he pets me untying my wrists to cradle me in his lap. Then using the small of my back he gathers me in his arms crying himself to sleep. I wait for his arms to slacken, for the breathing to roll out, watching the dust settle on the floor. I'm tired and my skin is peeling off me, there's a blue tinge and in the bathroom mirror I stand staring at my reflection.

I hear a noise turn my head to see Doll push open the door, she giggles and tucking her head out the door returns with a brush and sits me on the toilet lid brushing my hair. I watch her in the mirror my dark brown hair liquid through her fingers. My face mouth agape I see the corners of my lips stretch out. I smile at myself open my blue eye closing the other to look over Doll. Her crisp white uniform pressed the little hat held in with pins, I stand to

stroke her hair which she gives me the brush
motions for me to brush her hair her lips move
her eyes trailing mine.   Is she whispering? She
turns to unfold a gown and pants draping them
over the sink before kneeling down to slip my
socks off. Standing she unties the gown and
tosses it in the hamper I reach out to slip my
hand under the first button on her blouse I rest
it there and then pull it through I trail the edge
down the next button and pop it out before Doll
slaps my hand taking a surprised step back she
opens the door and stands holding it with her
other hand busily trying to re button her blouse.
Her face is red her lips tremble catching her
breath she smoothes her shirt pointing at me her
lips slowing puckering then eyes me cautiously.
She shuts the door leaving me naked in the
bathroom as I hear the lock click I turn inspect
the window find the crank handle still works I
close it up when I hear foot steps. I stand by
the sink as the door opens Birdie and Doll look
me over and quickly dress me. another cold
clear shot of pills chased by juice, I hold a few
under my tongue, pouching them to avoid
Birdie's visual inspection. They nod to each
other tuck me into the bed and turn off the
lights closing the door. spitting the three pills
into my hand inspect them only to find them
slightly dissolved into the pitcher by the bed I
drop all three turning the lid I finish dissolving

them and check for any residue before putting the pitcher on the night stand.

The nightstand next to the front door had two guns in it.

"Tell me " he whispers "tell me there are no others for you." He takes a long drag off the cigarette taps the ash onto my backside as he sits astride me. slapping my ear he demands an answer. My hands are tied behind me, he flips me over to face up at him and rests his weight on my hips. The cigarette is fresh and he sucks at it watching my face.

"I love you, every putrid inch of you. I would give you my heart from my chest. But you…" he slips his fingers around my jaw his lips twitching then he sighs. "so lucky, I know how lucky I am." He licks my crusty lips spits on them to lick them again it is a hot wet singe. I can smell a fiery tang, I can't feel my hands. He sits up scratching his chin. The few blonde stray hairs more fur than thatch line under his lip. Rubbing his teeth over my neck to my shoulder down my right side the way my toes curled as he bit me as he poured whiskey in my fresh wounds. I can hear hum breathing purring thunder as my heart wept as each stroke took my breath. As each word of his whimper began to disgust me. As he confessed his love over and over again, I began to hold my breath. I began to doubt his love.

He laid me out in the tub washing the dried blood from my lips and leaning over me I raised my hand slap his face he put his hand over my face pushing me down into the tub I slipped down to grab his wrist and pull him towards the tub. Over the edge I went using the lip to put my knees on his shoulders breaking the plain wooden chair underneath him. I twisted wrapping my thighs around his neck. His face and each pounding hand slowed my pulse, I watched his eyes darken steel between my wet legs. Slacked until he laid face up on the floor I stood stepping over him to walk down the hall I heard his first gasp I swung each arm lengthening my stride I felt his feet pound the floor behind me and sliding on my knees I rammed in to the hall drawer dumping the gun out and standing to point it at his chest. Spreading his legs he puts one hand on each side of the hallway stopping two feet nearly putting his chest against the muzzle. He ketches his breath then closes the gap resting his hands on my hips. I push the gun pulling the trigger feeling it click I pump through the rounds confirming it's not loaded. He shakes his head "mmmmm that's nice but a bullet is too easy. Why kill any one so far away?" he kisses my ear I push him back taking the warm gun to his face until he flings me into the wall. "Baby do you think you are hurting me with all this foreplay?" he snaps up the gun and a click through the chambers slowly counting random numbers until the last which he declares proudly thirteen.

It's a shrill cry, it's every breath forcing out my lungs, cracking my ribs. What else would I do but survive? This rolling over and playing dead it never saves me an inch of strength. The irritants of life are never deadlier then when your heart stops or when your chest no longer heaves. I feel the vowels spray the sky, the mud encasing me as I writhe pushing myself up to my feet . the water rising a wave cresting yards from my erect scramble. Plunging a few feet below the surface I swim with no knowledge of land, no need to look ahead, any way could be wrong.

It may sound desolate but there's no longer a true future not tainted by the taste of him. I can't strip myself of his love. I will take it with me. take it out as I awaken in the narrow bed, he's loading one gun as he unloads another switching the ammo between them kissing each bullet. "I could have shot you." as he nuzzles the loaded gun to my forehead. I turn my head letting it rest between my eyes and I stare at his baby blue eyes. There never was a future. hope can be a sweet fairy tale but he's not whispering about dandelions in my ear. We'll never hold hands at the movies, make out on a checkered blanket, and we'll never miss it. It sounds sticky. A gooey scorched coating, a life better exploited for profit than morality. Every time I wake up and I feel it on my skin and I want to pare off as many layers under it. I can't breath rubbing shoulders with the populous.

I can't convey all the depth of my selfish notions of honor and love. It's a different bond between he and eye he's still talking to me, his lips quiver but I can't hear his voice anymore. I feel the huff of his breath on my face, my back and my ear. His hands no longer linger over my chest or graze me. rarely does he sleep bedside me in the bed as I lay there listening to his shuffle step down the hallway outside the door. I think he doesn't sleep pacing caged around the house. I tethered to bed find my feet also bound, found myself sleeping through each pause in his company. Found myself alone with my thoughts. It feels dangerous to stroll through life waiting on death. I promised I wouldn't surrender to a life not as strong as my own. The hiss of a radio and I can sleep no longer the door stands open and coils of rope tempt me to slip a foot over the edge facing the door I slack the lead rope and free my hands crouching down I try to loose the ankle ropes. Too quiet much like and echo vibrates the floor.

My lips feel heavy crusty my mouth is dry the hallway is empty. I inch along the hallway towards the front of the house two steps then slide down letting my knees rest on the floor. My head is going to explode as my heart cracks another rib. I'm shaking wondering what will be next. My fingers tap the dark dusty wood floor and I try to ketch my breath. I think about Doll stroking my hair, her bosom soft against me with the scent of comfort. I close my eyes put my face on the floor the wood spins, I lay down knees to my chest. Where would I go? There's nothing else I want more than to have my passionate life. To have all the emotions rip me down nearly taking my life, my heart wants the thrill. My heart pushes my body it wasn't my mind that saved me and my heart is selfish. Why wait on a rescue? Every time I hit the floor I will rise back up smiling ready to take the next round. It does require more than hope can give me. There's nothing left as each stroke of his belt and each hiss in my ear have blared out a fury. A tide rising in me I stand up stepping into the kitchen empty and soft sunlight. I hear the front door turning to see him drop his bag of groceries to open the drawer pulling out one gun, pointing it at me his static deepens out I step into the gun my chest thrust out my hands out on my sides. I surrender give me death if you can no longer love me. I hear the click as the gun is empty, I turn to rip the drawer out and dump the other gun onto the floor. He's on me collapsing me on the gun it pushes on my ribs and my heart reaches for my throat. I'm vibrating the floor feeling how my breath rushes out my sealed lips. I pass out.

Double white snaps his fingers I sit startled wearing a thin gown. It itches and standing I pull it over my head. I fling it at Double white and turn towards the door I turn into a hallway taking a right before two orderlies appear filling the hallway. It's my breath I hear hard out my gaping mouth and I smile rubbing my mark. I sail into the orderlies who hold me as Birdie rounds a corner bearing a syringe, she taps it before instructing the men to lay me on the floor to be sedated safely. I stare at her shoes, black heels resting on blue tile. I watch her shadow as she leans down to arrange my arm. Her chirp a purr as she strokes my hand. It's her chirping, the bird at the window, and the slap of her wings on the glass, I'm tied to the kitchen stool letting my gaze burn holes in the glass. He's humming chopping carrots mincing them before dumping them into a pot steaming on the stove. I feel invisible. My weight is tethered to a handle of a drawer behind my back I sit up leaning against it before watching him. Shirtless his bald head and chest furry with blonde faint hairs, I can smell potatoes, blood and his aftershave. I lean forward pulling out the drawer as I land face first. Laying on the floor I turn watch his feet still faced away from me. His bare feet the edge of his jeans resting at the ankle as they shuffle between the fridge and the stove. The rope is still binding my hands but I stand up find myself dizzy collapse once again his heels inches away.

You can tell me about the American dream. Tell me how the pursuit of happiness is paramount to our culture. In context out of context what exactly makes it American other than the selfish singularity. Maybe I only wanted the dream. Can't wake up to the every day world pass among those crowded streets, trying to find myself useful for the tangible life. There are few things more powerful than these notions of freedom, despite dangerous consequences every heart sacrifices. He and I we slipped the every day, I fell reaching for him. He turns now over me inspecting the stitches. Tracing my mouth pushing the corners up smiling as he shakes his head. Brings me up onto my knees rests my face in his crotch as he stirs the pot. Taps it before stroking the back of my head after he rests the spoon on the counter. He pulls out a small pair of scissors from a drawer and cradling my chin

I jerk my face out of his hand as he rests the point on a thread. I look at the floor waiting to get slapped but he tosses the scissors back in the drawer sliding it closed. It's an eerie silence the pot bubbling as he drags the spoon through it. I close my eyes and rest my face on his thigh. He's singing but I can't hear him I only feel his chest vibrate see his lips move. I turn facing up to watch him. He smiles tapping the spoon as he belts out a tune. Stroking my head before rolling my face into his groin he palms the back of my skull and down my neck across my shoulders bending over me his fingers along my bones. I want to hear him. Hear him sing to me again.

It's Doll though she fills my nostrils before I open my eyes peering at her bosom as she leans over me. Sickly sweet today but not ripe, a gentle intoxication, her breast tucked beneath a few layers of cloth I open my mouth hear the fabric scrap. Doll straightens up clearing her throat then turns leaving the room. Idle time spent with my own thoughts often unhinges me before, with and after him. My skin prickles it is unsettling to not know what comes next. I'd rather not entertain any possible futures for fear of failure. For fear of delusion that these details and events become a reality of their own. What if I spend more time with my thoughts and less coping with the challenges of modern life? It feels irresponsible but modern life seems forced, mechanical. A life for those able to hold their thoughts, those not burdened by uncertainty. The bed creaks as I sit up, Doll shuts the door. It's a small room and there's only one door. The window's glow is fading, maybe it will be night soon. I watch the glass grow dark listening to the hum of the building. I lay over my knees resting my head on my shoulder, eyes still trained on the window.

I'm looking for the little bird but I remember seeing it bash It's head into the glass smearing half the pane. The window here is much larger but frosted section in quarters my head aches filled with silence I let out a long sigh. The hiss startles me and sitting up my right leg jerks. My eyes clear as I cough slipping to the edge to dangle my feet the floor is a few inches away it feels clammy my feet magnets drawing me down. I stand listen for my breath drawing in, put my hand over my lips dry soft I blow on my fingers exhaling through the Cheshire cat grin. His body might still be a few floors below me toe tag dressed, I step towards the door my ear to the wood. The handle gives I slide into the hallway shutting the door behind me taking a glance down the shorter corridor I see doors shut looking for one with a heavier handle I see a sign for the stairway. The large push bar pops I quickly step into the landing pulling it closed behind me. There's a door marked roof access and stairs leading down. My stomach gurgles I sit on the first tread downward closing my eyes. I am a woman without direction, without control beyond my heart's will to survive. It's epic each time life stole my breath away but each time my heart burst tougher after in the ruins. I live as if I can afford to give it all away. I don't find it precious but fearless. I stand lowering my foot onto the next stair picking up speed as I loosen up my legs. I clear my throat quivering as I let go of the rail to walk down the third flight of stairs. I hear muffled noises from the door marked 4 the shadows flicker under it. I place my hands on the door turning to feel the hum then continue on feeling the night air infiltrate the lower floors. The basement doors have large windows frosted and the night chirps nearly wrapped around me. I touch my bare thighs under the gown knowing that being spotted will inhibit departure. Standing a few minutes I return to the 4 door opening it gingerly relieved at the dusky light of the hallway seeing no one around I find a laundry hamper filled with dingy blue scrubs. I pull on pants standing there in the dim nearly holding my breath I put the gown in the hamper and pull on a shirt. Back in the stairwell I let out my breath rest remove the socks and walk barefoot down the stairs returning to the basement door. In the frosted pane I see my brown hair dark shaggy over my eyes. The blue eye white as I brush my bangs over it before swinging the door out to find a parking garage. There's a man having a cigarette standing next to a white van. "you are not wearing shoes." He says taking a drag before adding "kind of a sloppy escape" he puts it out and steps towards me I turn to run towards the ramp leading out of the garage. My hands flung forward as I punch finding the pavement hot before feeling the man's fingers on my legs sending me face first into the ground.

I spit blood at the man's face when he spins me around to carry me over his shoulder. Rubbing my face into his back he flips me back to the ground slapping me twice before putting his finger in my face as I pucker up to cover him in bloody spit. His backhand is much harder and my lips curl into a smile. "you are a sick bitch 13" he backhands me one more time before putting me over his shoulder to return to the staircase. Adjusting my weight he climbs the stairs back to the 3rd floor. As soon as he pops the door nurses spin around from the hallway I kick at him and he flings me to the floor stepping away as the nurses approach. I lay on the floor eyes open letting my mouth

135

hang open. None of the nurses has touched me they hover a foot away three of them conferring heads nodding until one is chosen. She lets out her breath and puts a finger to my throat declaring me alive before puling a pen light from her pocket. I hear a click.

He loads one gun four rounds then dumps some or all out, I can't see him. I can only hear the clanking of the metal. There's no rhythm and he's not singing, he's crying sobbing softly. I hear a click and he laughs then I feel the gun against my back. He lays it over my shoulder then the other as wings. The tips resting close to my spine. Then from over my shoulder he puts the tip in my face kissing my ear as he pulls the trigger 'click.' I keep asking how did I survive each day that did not go my way? Then I began to remember allowing days to slip by uncounted, the sun, the moon and even the stars feel alike in between the closing of my eyes. I blink, I blink hard drawing a tear wetting my cheek. When was the last good day? The one that made it worth while? Maybe one bearable enough to remember. What is it about each day of life that is delightful enough to want every day?

I'm closing my eyes looking for the backs of my memories. Testing the scent in the wind trying to remember what home feels like as I feel the needle fill my vein. I know such sweetness as the grass lays over my limbs. I smell my hands. Lick the mud from a finger. They loom golden. I can't bring the words together, can't let it rise up my throat, I haven't a word to give the air even in sacrifice. My heart it screams wails a banshee ripping the vines from my limbs, I'm torn and a hiss raspy along the river. I sway with the grass standing naked, the mud drying in the moonlight. My hands out stretched the lightning flashing in a seeping hot night. The crickets come to a rest pause then roll on, my hand over my mouth. How would you contain nothing?

I trail my arms out in front of me, the grass waist deep, I look out over the field trying to see to the horizon in the distance nothing glimmers. I sit down stare into the grass listening beyond each note. Where will my feet take me? how can I escape this place as well? My condition never seems to improve I am some how invisible but not unlucky enough for misery not to find me. I know this day with in a day. I know I'm dreaming but I'm held there turning around in circles unable to step forward. Forward is only an action and I put both hands over my mouth feeling my face. Then over my bare chest I drop my left arm when my right index finger slips over the scar. I smile hoping to light up the night drifting around me. There is no escape. I feel a thud,

land on my back look up at the ceiling with
Doll's face concerned her mouth puckered a
bit. She takes a wash cloth wiping my face.
It's sweet her voice soft muffled humming
keeping time with the tap of her toe. Then I
hear the music a trumpet moons over the loss of
the piano's tremble. As she opens her mouth
it's a sour glaze pouring over each lip her pity
is rotten my nose wrinkles up, Doll puts the
washcloth away sitting up. Her eyes well up as
she throws open her mouth to gloss the heavy
words before her head tucks into her shoulder
as she wipes her face on her sleeve. Rising she
gathers up the bowl and cloth returning them to
a cart before wheeling out of the room.

　　　　The wheels squeak as they hit the
hallway tile. He's laying on me I can smell
him. Draped over my back he stirs rolling off
me to resettle a foot away. I turn feeling the
rope around my ankles I sit up to survey the
room. Dusky, it might be a new day or an out
going one, he does not stir as I bring my ankles
closer to my hands his face away from me only
the ridge of one shoulder pushed up. I tug the
rope see it taunt to the foot rail. I nudge the
knot feeling it tighten then decide to slide down
the bed to find the end. Turning to pause as I
kneel at the foot rail, he mumbles in his sleep
then slumbers on. The rope goes under the bed
I can't reach far enough to find the end even

over the side. But the knot loosens with the slack I work it off each ankle revealing a purple indention. I finger it caressing my pale leg then rolling over the side of the bed I kneel watching his mass rest on the bed.

I think about the depth of his timber and how he sings pausing then adding in his own words for the ones he forgot. His trembling lip and the way he would sneer to settle it. The silence sweats my skin as I stand over him turning to open the door before watching his feet resting my hand on the knob. His belt on the floor still through the belt loops I lean down taking the buckle off before freeing the worn leather. I bend it in half raising it over my head poised over him when I see his left eye come open, his hand on my chest as I fling my arms down striking his out stretched hands. The door holds my weight as he pins me on it bending to retrieve the belt he steps back. Both his eyes are open regarding me his silence unravels me and I throw my fists against his chest while he wraps his arms around me. Defeat, always maybe never I don't have a plan. This day has come around the same as any other. I haven't failed because I haven't stopped my pesky heart from beating. His love is worth nothing but then again nothing is easier to contend with. He takes me down the hall to the bath room filling up the tub and we both get in the tub. Humming while he cleans my lips, shaves my body and the warm water is pink. He holds me his eyes wet and using the wash cloth washes those tears away. I run my hands over his face cover his left eye. I want to lick his right socket. I want a white blue eye.

A crack of thunder awakens me in the blue bed all alone hearing the rain crest the pavement I sigh hold my lips close. This day, that day none of it has really mattered in the slope of my life. I gave into the notions of reality but held onto the delusions of grandeur. Not one sweet note can be forever. I slip out of the bed the door is locked and the window sealed. I am a prisoner of my thoughts. The floor it's cold and every step leaves mist. I'm looking myself over undressing taking off the gown, the underwear, and gnawing at the plastic looped around my wrist. It tastes heavy perfume I tug on it with my other hand. What should I be doing here? Is he floors below me or ashes in the prison yard? I squat down kneeling to look under the door but it's seated well and even light barely passes. I straighten up to lay my ear on the steel. My heart throbs filling my lungs rattling the door a fine spray of my breath as I think about his kitchen floor. Looking down into the hallway waiting for his feet to appear then jumping up gun in hand as he stands his arms in the air puts the nuzzle in his chest. There isn't a round in the gun but I squeeze it over and over again letting it click watching his face. Staring me down a smile creeps over his face he takes the gun and slaps my face throwing me into the wall. I slide down to my knees as he steps around me. The gun clunks into the drawer against the one that might be loaded. Slamming the drawer he returns behind me, pulling me down to the floor to rub his groin in my face. He grunts drool down his lip. Tells me I'm stupid, how he should have never fucked me. Now he's stuck with me because I would like death too much. The other girls were a waste but you " you 13 are a monster" he drags me back to the bed ties me limbs spread out. I'm watching him as he softly sings I can't hear the words but I hear him whispering. His head shaking side to side as he lips out the words a heavy piano falling on my face I shut my eyes.

I'm waiting but the world feels pulled away. There's a current but I can't hold it. It runs up my chest and I shake as each finger stretches out. I'm swaying right here without any steps I'm trying to open up my breath and see what tomorrow will bring for me. I haven't a hope and sometimes not a care. I'm watching massive amounts of illusions peel back the most selfish desires of ego. This breath aches my organs, this breath weighs me to the ground. Those nasty little pieces of my flesh they ache and twitching I know I need to survive my self.

I long to be with him even in ash. I think of him is this weary head laying it down on the cold tile and cry. My mouth gaping open shaking to roll my head back to pry a word even a letter from my teeth. It's no good. The air is thick with dust. My eyes slat open as I see a gloved hand holding a mask over my mouth and nose. I open my mouth pulling in the air to open my eyes. It tastes like bad strawberries and I snarl up my face trying to gap the mask. The hand moves to maintain the pressure I feel a hand stroking my hair. I am beyond tired as my limbs disappear I open my eyes trying to find a face beyond the hand.

I'm not sure if anything I know is certain. What if my skin becomes foreign and I alienate my flesh then will I howl out a sound? Will I crest the atmosphere with screams rippling the fabric of night? I can't hold on and so I escape into air. But it's only a breath as I step into the hall shutting the door behind me then running my nails down it's length I hear him roll out of the bed his footfalls heavy and quick as I lean my weight on the door. His weight stopping short of the panel, his breath hard as he gulps turning the knob. I close my eyes I want to see his face I step back from the door opening my eyes to him nose to nose. His huffing breath as he lets go of the knob to back hand me. I smile the running drip of blood cold on my chest. Grabbing my shoulders he licks the blood spot sucking at my breasts and biting as I gaze at the ceiling. I close my eyes I can hear him groaning. I can hear him calling me. Telling me how painful it is to love me.

It's my soul discolored as rotten or parasitic, it's this heart rocking in my chest whining out through my twitching muscles. I pursue ever darker passions. I can hear the crickets so many a mild buzz laying here in a bed. I want to lick my lips I think about it and run my fingers over my lips stretching each one opening my eyes when I complete the circuit. Grey ceiling a soft night with me and the crickets. It's dry and I cough muffled by my right hand. Bring my left up to sit up looking at a closed door. I long for the night's sky to smell the open air. Nothing moves the crickets lucid as I begin to twitch. I fold the blanket back count my toes flex them, pop my fingers counting them. My bones feel solid I can stand up without holding the bed. The cold floor quivers my legs I search the two drawers for socks. The bible still in plastic Gideon can't aide me. I have to continue on my way. I go to the door it opens outward the hallway darker falling lighter on the right. Left I hug the wall adjusting to the dark as I open a closet door I change into faded green scrubs put little booties on my naked feet. There's a hamper and I check each article of clothing until I feel a plastic square badge still clipped on the neck of Double White's jacket. It falls down my chest as I clip it picture towards me. I take a breath and step into the hallway to pass the lighted desk down the right. I intend to walk passed it to walk slow enough to find the exit. To find my way out of this day. It's quiet I let my breath out swallow as the hallway becomes filled with light. I stand a few feet from elevators stepping up to them I push the down button. It lights up but does not ding or bell when the doors open. Safely inside I turn around to face the closing doors on Birdie's face gazing downward behind the desk. There are 5 floors below me and no basement I choose 1, it has a star next to it. I bounce a little as the doors open into another hallway I step out it's dim but not dark. I see glass to the left and stride down the darker hallway hearing doors sliding open and the crickets barreling hiss. It's concrete under my feet as I step through the door turning to gaze upward I stand taking it in. The crickets although many, no longer intertwine into a buzz, whisper to me as I look over the parking lot deciding. There's no more him in my ear telling me about his love. There's no more him.

I stood there crying as I began to cross the parking lot. I dried my tears on the borrow clothes I began to think about the world outside and stopping on the far sidewalk I turned around. This isn't a world for me. The air feels good and I watch the sun rise after climbing the small hill in the fenced lot beside the hospital. I move to where I can see the doors I came out of I'm not sure what to do but I'm curious. Up a tree I find a spot I can see the glass sliding doors open. But the tree shakes and a man starts screaming at me. I skid down hitting the ground as he tells me "don't climb the trees now you are covered in pesticide." He takes out a card with instructs on how to get the poison off. Hands it to me and then stepping back " you really shouldn't be in here. Did you climb the fence?" I nod and he takes out keys turning to lead me out. I follow holding the card as he takes me to the edge of the hospital parking lot opens a gate and then walks me back to the hospital he walks me down to another desk and leans on it telling a girl behind it that he's brought her a tree climber. She giggles and reappears from a door to lead me down a hallway. Opening another closet door she tells me "she only has the regular scrubs and not the fancy ones I'm wearing "but she has my size. Then grabbing up slippers as she inspects my feet. We walk further and she gives me a bottle and a sponge. " take as long as you like make sure you strip down completely I gave you an under shirt with shorts." Opens the door into a shower room she presses the button and closes me in.

How long will this freedom last? I strip down pushing the clothes down into the hamper keeping the badge. I'd start at the beginning but it's somewhere I've never been. It's a constant pressure to worry over fine tuning when the instrument doesn't exist. I exist despite how easily I become invisible to others. I carry on calm at the boiling but unwound in the ease of any given day. Hands shake and I fight my nerves twitching while I lean in the adjust the temperature of the shower. My healed lips, the glow of my skin as I smell the soap before pouring it on the sponge. It's clear nearly odorless but faint the lemon as I lather up. Under my left breast his mark still stains the rough patch makes me smile.

My head is heavy the inability to sleep has squeezed my brain these flying days will bring a nice crash. I will lay down to quell this throb. Me, myself and I have been rolling out the pain bringing my hysterics upon themselves. I came thus far. The night has always been mine and flowing the ripples of vice shall suffice these itches to swish death in my glass. I am a rising woman taking my turn in every tingling moment. There's a price, every breath dangerous, every full step forward a possible slide backward. Do I know how not to fail? Is the secret of humanity the ability to allow these chronic miseries to not steal the joy even in the face of tragedy? It is not a lack of faith in my spirit. It is not the crimson purple of my flesh or the sweat of my brow but the strength of my will. I will survive.

The water slips over my face despite what the girl said I'm sure I can't stand in the shower much longer. I study my blue eye in the mirror as I dry myself. Little tears down my arms where I held the tree as I lifted myself into its limbs. I could be anyone right now anywhere. I could be Jessica, Stephaney, or Eloise, even Heather but there isn't a name beneath my numbered chest. My heart beat, it's faint push on the pads of my fingers, right hand spread under my left breast I stand there naked seeing, feeling the new shape of me. Seeing history leak out over skin pale olive the blue eyed glows white I can't help smiling my lips parting slightly. I'm tired overcome with sore aches. I collapse face down on the grey tile floor.

I'm lying in the tub my face below the water line as I open my eyes seeing him over me. His hands on my chest his weight in the palms spread over my ribs. I am still, watching his image dance, a sway ripple and then the he pulls the plug beneath my shoulder blade. The water uncovers my face and I let it run from my mouth as he turns me to rest my head on the side. My eyes are open I try to not look him in the eye. I stare at his chest, his slim figure as the jeans, soaked with bath water, are black. He turns to the sink I see the syringe and I can't move as he sucks the liquid up tests the plunger and kneels down beside the tub. The warmth returns to my skin making the needle a cold sting as it draws out. He turns away I leap over the edge hitting my shoulder into him knocking him to the ground. I scramble pushing up from all fours to develop traction on wet tile. My right foot trapped by his hands I see the hallway before landing only inches from the door. On my back I see him grab both ankles to drag me closer. He laughs sitting astride my hips. Slaps my face the first hit fuzzes the room. I sway I know it's the flat of his hand tilting me and then I raise my hand fist into his cheek. He pins my hands down letting the drool and blood roll down his lip as he leans his face in to wipe it on my cheek. It's hot rolling down my jaw his fingers spread over my throat as he pulls me to my knees. My hands fanned over the floor feet tucked under my ass. He looks down at me, face in his crouch legs pressed into my ribs.

It's my heart hot loud in my ear every muscle takes the cue and from the floor I push up his frame knocking him into the tub. I fall back turning to crawl to the hallway before rising to climb the wall. In the living room I stop over the drawer next to the door laying my hand on the handle I listen for him. I crouch kneeling in front on the drawer sliding it out as I look into it both guns. I pick up both guns and see the bullets covering the bottom of the drawer. I feel the floor quiver and turn seeing him slam into my waist he lands on me a gun still in my left hand I use my elbow and knee him in the chest. He grabs my thighs thumping the wind out of me before I back hand him in the face the gun cutting his bottom lip. He shakes his head licks his bloody lip looks up at me spitting before smiling. The gun in his face I pull the trigger every click he licks his lip. It's empty the other gun isn't in sight he's crawling toward me he takes the gun flinging it across the living room next to the other one. I dare not take my eyes off him as he puts his face on my leg licks my calf his teeth nibbling my thigh. I turn my head the blue of his eyes is caught in the dim overhead light. I close my eyes feeling him kiss my thigh his teeth gnaw at my skin. He stands before taking me over his shoulder and back to the bed. It's the floor I hit first. It's a folding house of cards my limbs seems separate I pile on the wood. He's still breathing heavy wearing the black now sweat soaked jeans they fall on his hips and I wonder where the belt has gone. I wonder if it's day or night.

I hear the birds cawing heavy at the window their wings filling out the pane. Rich black dipped silver by what could be a pale moon. A rattling wind his breath evening out as he binds my hands in prayer I, on my knees, smell his blood still fresh on his lip. I pinch his lip squeezing hard as he slaps my face landing me onto the floor. The floor stings I turn trying to push out my bound hands away from his calf. He kicks my ribs and pulling me up to my knees hauling me by the rope around my hands. I drag limp, gravity's victim, as he tries to lift my face to look at him.

It doesn't matter what I see. It doesn't matter what I hear. The air is pungent, death obscuring my orifices. Covered in it as I breathe it my bones jutting out the folds of skin dripping melted down into hell. A body can survive stripped but I must inquire about its true form. I must ask about necessity. Consider the mechanics involved, I'm not going do more than protect myself from death. How long? How long will it continue? How much torment? These truths are not so much greater as basal. I turn my eyes locked on his. The snarling white fogging the seeping blue it could drip down his face. I thrust up push my face into his the cheek bone popping before I return with gravity his hand following my descent. The slap becomes a rhythm between his yelling a fury sweeping my face. I fall to the floor stare up at him his mouth open chest sharply rising huffing bent over me.

I can hear the heart monitor. Body turning under the cotton blanket, ping rest ping steady I blink I taste plastic, I taste dull metal. I sit up pull the tubes from my nostrils wiping the goo blowing my nose filling my lungs coughing up more goo. " I love you" I hear him saying it echoing in the cement as I slide off the bed face down unable to grip the blanket. I see swirling blood in the gobs from my face all over my hands I sit back against the bed pulling the sheets down wrapping myself knees up tight staring at the door. Ridiculous I wipe my face with the sheet edge and dry my eyes. My nostrils burn but if I stopped rubbing them they drizzle. I get up go to the door. It's locked and window less, the window that faces the door is big but has many sections. I can't stand to hear him say 'I love you' the soft slush. Putrid churning in my stomach my guts tightening at each word drawn out over his lips.

I'm staring a staring at his face. His dull grey eyes over me and the silence rustles in my mouth. I'll always want him, even taste him through my blood. It's the sweetest thing, my sickest desire is a freedom from the parental needs of governing bodies. Allowing ,e the inhumanity of selfish destruction. I can't feel any joy in the procreation of this species. In my breath perhaps I taste the whims of reality. My organs, my flesh and my skin belong to no one, not even me. inching onward taking my hands around his throat the blood running down my cheek from my lips. Each slap of lanky flying fingers failing to turn my head.

I sit up, a cold sweat as I stand at the door listening to the silence on the other side until feet draw up the hallway. I smile my hand on the handle waiting for the loud steps to halt. I look up see a window at the top of the door hear the steps march away. it's open turned outward, the dust is thick and the chair brings me a foot from the gap. The pane is stuck in it's angle barely moving as I tug and push the frame. The hallway is dark down one side. The other only a few feet before being lit by the nurse's station several more feet away. I jump off the chair to the floor testing my balance and listening for movement after the thud of my weight.

Nothing. My heart beat as I ripple a smile across my face I get back on the chair and pull myself up to see if I can get through the window. I rest my belly on the pane turning over I put my hands through the ceiling panels for a beam. Slide my legs then looking down the lighted hallway I drop to the floor.

Nothing. My heart is swelling and the wild grin opens as I turn walking into the dark end. My eyes adjust and I locate the push bar of the stairwell door. it's dim lit by the pale light of morning I can smell absence on the concrete steps. The door closes behind me and I stand there looking out the window, from a few floors up leaning into the sill to look down. I take a deep breath and head down the first flight.

The future any day but this one. I'm not busy with any thing other than survival. These concerns about time beyond now would only cloud me from getting through this day. This day is hard enough and it never seems to end. Not repeating but scrawling out sputtering calamity and concurring chaos sparing me none of my emotions. I see a light in the third floor access door cautiously I open it into an empty but well lit hallway. There's a staff locker room the door is propped open. A wet floor sign inside it I step around. The room is empty the floor a few wet spots I kick the stopper on the door up and close it. Masking tape layered locks in the doors I frisk one finding the third one in open.

Nothing. The lower ones have scrubs stacked by size in separate lockers. Soft pale blue ratty edges I slip on a pair of pants tie the drawstring checking the opposite row of lockers I find white undershirts I fold the gown I was wearing find a shirt and tuck the gown under my arm. I find a shower in room behind the lockers and three pairs of sneakers. Lined up scrubbed white toes towards the wall they smell of disinfectant. I turn hearing the locker room door open and see a woman drop her bag on the long bench pop open a locker and hang her purse inside. Two other women join her, I lace up a pair of the sneakers. I walk out of the locker room not making eye contact with any of the women. I go back into the stairwell crouch down on the door to look downwards. Two maybe three more flights I step quicker hearing cars scratching as I come to the bottom door.

Nothing He slaps me and I lay on the wood. Crouching over me he braces my hands over my head slides them down to my shoulders I can't look at him. My head is turned to my right but I open my left eye to gaze at him. I can hear the crickets between his breaths hiss sweat rolls down his forehead. Wiping it with his forearm he gnashes his teeth drawing back his hand to lay another slap I hear it land. I hear it thump the floor but I turn to face him he leans back onto his heels grabbing my ankles to drag me down the hallway. A squelching slow slide my body turning as he loses his footing. I pull my legs under me and roll my body forward finding wood and rushing towards him I push his chest under my palms. On his torso I rest my weight as he coughs then regains his breath. We no longer struggle as the crickets even my heart rate. He runs his hands up my calves and then rubs my thighs watching my face. He sits up dumping me onto the floor his hands wrapped around my thighs. My shoulders rest on the floor the wet sticky residue of me staining the wood.

Nothing he stares at me between my thighs I watch him bow his head resting his mouth on my inner thigh. He opens his mouth wide showing me his teeth before biting down. I don't feel it and as he releases I see his lips move but I don't hear a sound not the crickets. Not my own heart beat, his breath or even the tick of time, in all of this cloud I watch him lick up my thigh lap at my crouch.

Nothing there are no cars in motion when I open the door. I walk to the first parked one trying the handle. Locked, I move on going across the row choosing a small truck with tarps in the back I climb into the bed and pull the tarp over me I feel tired. I listen to the crunch of gravel. The sporadic steps opening doors, starting engines. It smells of gasoline and I push my hand further under the tarp feeling a container the spigot removed. It's empty but the fumes are strong under the tarp I lay my head down close my eyes.

He's mopping the floor, bleach I can taste it while I sit in the bathtub. The water is pink and warm I slide my head down letting the water rise over my face I see his face appear and I sit up again my eyes fixed on him. Sitting on the toilet he takes out a needle fills it and pinching my hip pulling it out of the water to inject me. He slaps me a few times his teeth clenched. My head lobs over I feel rolled out, draped over the porcelain. I hear him leave the room the tile wet. His feet slap in a higher pitch then deeper as he enters the hard wood. I lay there listening to him mop side to side hitting the walls of the hallway then the bucket dragging further into the kitchen. I feel tears down my face but I am unable to lift my hands. There is no stopping time. There is no resolution. He returns his jeans wet from the bottom up a dark blue hanging on his hips. Sitting on the toilet again he doesn't look at me but stares out the window. A lost boy his blue eyes seeping grey he picks up the needle a few beads still cling inside he taps it then puts it in the cabinet. Back on the toilet he gazes at me removes his jeans his limp cock stuck to the pocket. Getting in behind me he lifts me up to settle me on his lap. I smell the bleach still strong on him, feel his warm body beneath my legs. With the washcloth he cleans my lips, wipes the tears from my face he begins to hum. The water shimmers in the fluorescent light, pink the soap all dissolved. He pets my head the new growth of my hair barely a centimeter. Kisses my ear down my neck whispering what must be the words to the song. The water goes cold his cock stays limp under me. We continue sitting in the bath watching the window darken until he pulls the plug bringing the towel in after the water disappears. He wraps me in the towel carries me to the bed. Dead weight in his arms the delicious sluggish slow warmth weighing me from my heart out. My heart beat is a ripple vibrating the sheet under me. His naked ass walking back to close the door before he lays down face to face with me. The towel is soft but he pulls it off me, rearranging my limbs, tossing it on the floor before returning to stroke my face. My hands begin to shake. I convulse feeling the tremble radiate from my innards. He rubs my shoulders he strokes my arms then puts his hand between my legs I feel him harden rubbing his crouch on me. Grinding my hip, licking my breasts his eyes closed his soft murmurs. There's nothing left to feel it's time slowing to a crawl in his arms, I close my eyes.

The truck shivers roaring to life I open my eyes stare up at the blue tarp holding the side as it lurches backward. To become a passenger, no longer driving the course of one's day. What is existence without the sound of life crawling across time? To assume one is alone, within my thoughts how could I not only find me. There is no argument about the betterment of mankind or the procreation of the species. I'm only after my own survival, my own bits of time. My mortality resting inside the marrow of a conscious notion. A heart's loud lungs, you are beyond the skin and sinew. The truck falls into rhythm gently rocking me. The crickets slow purr too cold for a summer night, the tarp still hauntingly warm.

He's tapping the bed frame, I laying with my head on his chest hear my heart rattle. Did I ever hear his heart intertwined with mine? Was he always dead inside? Maybe our loins made the summer longer insulating us from the world. Nothing lasts, time taught me that elapsing the years over my flesh. I wasn't a child forever and so never felt I would live much longer than my youth or strength or even the inclining of beauty. Life was the slope of my hips as fingers dug in. The nights shivering the inches of warm heaven revealing my bones. When I close my eyes can I not stop myself? I betray me. As he betrayed himself singing those sweet desires of a life few ever have, a life golden on paper, glossy sugar coated perfection. What could be happy would only crust my lingering thoughts. It's my wet face on his chest as he pushes me to the floor leaning over the side I don't look at him. Can't hear his breath but feel the huff between what must be the words he's shouting. I'm inside myself a place I never should open, a place filled with rage. My upheaval over a dream folding my nightmares over each day. I turn head towards the door pull my legs under me to stand crouching for a few quick steps. Clearing the door frame I slip in the dust feel his weight behind me but grazing the hallway wall I tumble into the living room. See him crash down on my belly the air knocked out button to back. My hands on his face slapping him balled up into his chest. Blood out his nose he falls back as I over take him astride his chest I pummel his fair face. Then caressing the crimson pooled on his upper lip dripping down his face. Sandpaper staining my hands he lets me rub it down his chest, it begins to dry under his nose. I backhand him once hard across his face I stare into his eyes the grey an emptiness. I put my right palm over his left eye closing my

right, balancing to lean in nose to nose.
There's nothing to look for knowing that these
moments are over too. These pauses, he's but a
pile of crushed dust. I lay beside him holding
his hand shoulder to shoulder the drawer only a
foot from my outstretched digits. Neither of us
moves the room's dingy light glows in the
kitchen swirling the settling clock. I ache to
make no decision. To allow life's motion it's
own erratic pulse. I sit up closer to the door
pull open the drawer take out one gun hear him
sit up. With the gun in my lap, I sit facing him
my knees in front of me folding each foot in to
keep the gun. He does the same and I take the
gun in my right pointing it to my temple. His
eyes widen as I pull the trigger not hesitating to
continue after each click. This gun is empty, I
backhand him with it letting it fly from my grip
and scratch the kitchen floor. He doesn't turn
his face back to me continues to stare eyes
closed. I grit my teeth reach into the drawer
picking up the other gun. Place it in my lap
waiting for him to face my again. I pound the
floor with the flat of my palms his face
squishing up with each thud. Squinting hard I
stop leaving both hands spread out on the wood
as his left eye comes open then eyeballing me I
pick up the handle once again to my temple this
time he bites his lower lip. His breath sucked
inward I pull the trigger. Several empty clicks

both these guns are empty his mouth grins leaning forward to put his hands on my face he licks my blood smeared face lips to eye.

I push him away using my fists as he kisses my shoulders shakes me before thrusting my back to the floor. Splitting my legs he chews my ear grinding his hips, his hardening member throbs gooey up my thigh. His grunting growl tells me the excitement is over I can not control my death. I can not escape his need.

Love is the harshness of my soul, an un kept acre where my heart wanders. The hunger doesn't belong to my heart. Further in my body the fiery ache resides. My love needs no excuses, tramples all organs, drawing up devouring to call out into the darkness. Wordless, thoughtless wonder please relieve me. Please release me from the pining of flesh. It never goes away despite the promises of my lips or the intentions in the gravel dipped knees praying for mercy. My howling carcass misses the brutality in passionate rapture. I have heard of love soft whispering as it lifts the heart. This sours the atoms I wince can't tolerate love without its evils, it's dark sludge. Love should be a beauty with all its hollow pain. A passion consuming every morsel of flesh, every ounce I will not confess. My will is violence. My heart never rests. If death is the answer then life was the question.   I'll take my chances with my will.

He leaves me on the floor to retrieve the guns from the kitchen and then dumping them into the drawer, slamming it shut he walks into the kitchen lighting a cigarette as he gazes out the window. Where are the bullets? I didn't feel them in the drawer nor hear them rattle.

To come down or go over the edge? Push the thresh hold , take a dive to avoid the crash. Everybody crashes even when the hurdle barely rises over the pavement. Somehow these little missteps become the undoing. I couldn't tell you about my own hurdles at least not their size. The one's I passed seemed huge as I closed in and tiny while I stumbled over them. Waste and excess, those hallmarks of the ideals of moderation. I can't measure the value of life. I loved all the fierceness of his love but felt shame at his mercy. The tender slips of his tongue, it was a sourness I longer to spit out. None of it's important. Screwed up perception. If I'm sick I'll embrace it. It shouldn't come as a missed opportunity but a careful acknowledgement of my differences. I am hand in hand created across the choices and circumstances of all the days behind. As for the days ahead there never was any doubt. My bare feet still hold my weight and every step forward can only lead somewhere new.

My fingers as I check my lips. That thread wet hot throb today is another day but where is this day? I'm sitting on the stool in the kitchen. He's waving his hands around chest puffed out, eyes blue, so blue I'm swimming, he slaps my face a few times. I don't feel it, see my vision swing looking down at his feet. His bare feet, his jeans stained rusty red I put out my hand touching his thigh. Off the stool into the cabinet but I swing, back handing him across the face. He smiles raising his hand I stare at the blue, a grin spread over his face he closes his right eye, I watch his hand fly towards me and straining the stitches I smile.

My blood feels rotten in my mouth. I smell, a corpse dragging its weight through a corridor searching. Dead but hungry. What words could I possibly defend myself with? No gravity in justification my lips snuggly sewn. What grief could I have over the tiles of his kitchen? My face down admiring the texture. The bleach strong in my nostrils. I believe it's all clear now. A shock of white spitting out his eye into my temple the whole heavy breath. His mouth hanging open frame by frame a millions eons as he calls out my name. It's a hard crack popping the air from my lungs but I rise up. Begin throwing things from the countertop cutting board wet. Slap and snap over his shoulder but with my feet under me I push off from the counter wrapping my legs around his throat taking my hands on the upper cabinet to pull his face into my crouch. He gasps for air closing his eyes hands searching for a drawer, pulling one out spilling cutlery on the tile. I open a cabinet grip the shelf find it fall into me as I try not to buckle his mass under me. I look up to grab the sides of the cabinet a heaving glass bowl smashes my left hand. Tumbling our limbs spread over his back. I grab the bowl lift it over and in mid air I pause to listen. My fingers pinch his shoulder then slip under feeling for warm mist. I hold my breath and slip back daring to not take my eyes off his face down sprawl.

Pause, looking for the end unraveling, patting my skin down over the course of hours thinking it is this inch that itches? Is this nerve going raw? Will this hand be enough to hold it together? As I throw it over my mouth, will I not fall forward unable to look the future in the eye? I'm wet rolling my body down the floor pushing my toes down standing to push him back. His face thick with softening gloss. I let it hurt, let it tear me down, my heart ripping out my throat. It stole my breath his fingers on my neck, my hands around his wrists. One hard breath while he pets my artery before spanning my jaw, his fingers tapping my windpipe. He regards me right eye open as I close my left he spits in my right it stings. I shake him off closing the left to recoil. He pushes back sending me a hard six inches of wood into the wall. My back is to him I feel his hands on my shoulders dragging me down the hallway a few feet before laying on my upturned hip.

We can talk bout the past as it's the future. The grievances popping up red flags we missed the first time. Make attempts to be proud of our bravery, our survival, to some how refuse the responsibility of the occurrences all together. I can't shrug off my existence despite the missing years or crawling days. The hours of strained silence it all belongs to me. Only me I'm not in his head, nor in his heart for the words from his lips fall silent on me, I feel his lips brushing my ear. His warm dry tongue flicking my cartilage. I open my eyes the wall inches from my face he gathers me up into his arms to deposit me on the bed where he secures me on my side facing the wall. His shadow blending with mine I feel the needle and close my eyes waiting for butter to fill me. Carry me out these pores find the birds out floating over the fields. Ripples waters rising the sludge between my toes the dry scratch of his face over the slight hip bone left out of the new chord. His teeth as I feel his jaw wet on my thigh. Nothing lasts forever.

The truck crunches to a stop, I hear the driver slam the door walk over around the bed and open another door. It slams and the crickets are with me in my stirred huff. I inch out from under the tarp stand momentarily at the tale gate before walking down the gravel driveway. Dusky dawn with a chill in the air I head toward the empty abandoned parking lot barefoot in the hospital scrubs I see a clothes line in the distance behind a broken picket fence. It takes a few minutes but I easily fit between the planks and scanning the yard before pulling a pair of jeans and a button up shirt off the line the pair of sneakers are too small and I leave them as I hop over the lower chain link fence on the opposite side of the yard. I can see the highway, mountains beyond it. The sun is clearing out the clouds as I walk towards the highway. I begin to hear trucks ambling down the two lanes. Once bright green the signs are more silver leaving out letters in their listed destinations. One could say I've never had a choice. One could say my rotten luck and poor timing led me astray. That I could still be a golden girl a lovely vision of polite society. Had I only been more careful, had I only heeded the dangers more proactively? Had I played it safe? As I walk deciding to head along the highway to see if it winds closer to the mountains I smile. I cover my lips still fingering the scars. The semi's down the road throw gravel back into the ditch I slide down the side sitting my head level with the top. I watch the day wave the pavement hiss the mirages further in the ribbons of blacktop. Where ever I go will be a long walk. The distance isn't illusive , the danger is in sitting here by the side of the road instead of traveling it. As if my past could chase me. As if there was an ago that would be again. A day that reappears unable to move on. I want to lay in the ditch be at the mercy of the terrain but I walk along it trying to step on the flatter rocks. Listening to the miles of road the tires push behind them while I sift through breaths. I can't recall his face only the thick husk in the leaking days running over my spine. I put my fingers in my mouth find myself skipping down the ditch slow as my right selects the rocks. I stop to stare up at the sun, then laying down face up I listen to the wind kick over the ditch hoping for clouds, hoping for rain to pelt my face. Trying to take the joy of survival from me, laying my right hand over my chest I slip two fingers under between the buttons stroking his brand.

      The ceiling over the bed was distant as if I could never reach up so high. I never stretched out my fingers to touch the dim corners of my vision. I lay there stroking his face running my fingers through the velvet beard on his cheeks. Petting the beast while he inhaled my dirt. If he licked a finger I would slap him grinning he let me slap him four times before returning the slap. He cleared his throat inspecting my lips examining my face, licking it, slobbering if I pulled away. wiping his face on my chest content with my stillness thumping my ribs with the flat of his hand watching to see if I squirm. I know the tide as it pulls my body through the cycles of the moon, pain rises instead of clinching, instead of turning away, and I roll into this wave. Ride it through my bones let it throb to an easy sigh. I eyeball him both eyes wide watching his lips curl into a smile as I lay each of my hands on my ribcage, palms cupping the arch of my torso. I can smell his musk as he cups my left breast in his mouth then moving my hands off my sucks the crusty scar forming on my brand. I tremble twitching vibrant under his furry face. I put my hands over his soft head grab his ears pull his head up. He resists biting the soft under arms until I begin slapping the side of his head. I land face up on the floor. I roll over and turn taking a knee out the door. Hitting the wall his weight pins me only two steps further.

I want to run a mile my bones nee a barbwire scratch as I twitch laying my hands on his chest. I would stroke his lips and he would take his fingers into his mouth grinning the right eye closed. I'm not holding still standing next to him in the kitchen his chest pressed against mine. A breath he intakes my air he lands on top of me on the wood it smells rancid. I am filled with poison leaking from my pores. The walls stained in the hallway I embraced them left my prints, left not one nail in the plaster. I hold out for a pause let my lungs rest in his arms. It's not a perfect tranquility. A loud ripple of sound his panting between the thuds. My face it stings but I see his face, the red pink cloud is he draining of color or radiating it? I slip my hand over the days old stubble faintly red at his check.

Who is this now and when did it ever matter? I find myself pooled over the glint of his eye but unable to see the color. Unable to feel his hand around my throat until I am blacking out. This tedium will not continue. It was never yes or no, it was still. It was the next breath, my next thought, impulse, and the need to survive. The question, there is never one, never simple and hardly deliberate. Those bridges I burned were all the days behind me in his arms. It was too late when I saw him. Too late when I smiled. We went together. We departed the status quo much earlier. The only destiny is death. I know it. the same as I know sweet honeysuckle in summer drifting over the lawn. Stars, hard and cold beyond my reach in the sky. He and I, laying in the ditch it is only I. I smile.

How far can anyone run? Regardless of the bounds of walls and the expanses of time there are only so many corners. What am I missing? You already know what comes next. It's still a love story. I still love him even through the broken bones. Or possibly around them it's melancholy and divine his eyes a murky blue. I know the tune as his head sways mouth open I don't know the words, I listen fixed on lips. Trying to pry words from air as he throws his head back eyes closed. It's useless as my ribs rock under his thighs. His love his chest brushing mine as he sings words in my ear then rises up to sway eye to eye smiling. I can feel his tenor vibrate his chest, his weight rock me I lay my head back to close my eyes. Feel him lick my throat and I roll forward dumping him on the kitchen floor rising pushing him against the cabinet. The door gives, he turns pulling it off its hinge I turn plowing my shoulder into the corner. Waiting as the crack of wood takes my breath I open my eyes and hands forward pull myself onto the counter turning feet under me to face him standing one chunk of the split door in his right hand. My fingers are wrapped around the lip of the yellowing slab I watch him. heavy breath he pulls up his air hard quivering the right nostril then striking the counter next to me the chunk pops once, then twice I look to his face he smiles slapping the wood a few more times huffing each time. I look back at the wood the drawer beneath it out an inch but it gets caught by his harder blows flipping down empty on the floor. I watched the drawer, missing him swing the wood to my face and down to the floor I land shoulder pushing me up. I curl finding myself blinded by the buzzing fluorescence. Screeching my hands catch his wrists. I turn my hands hitting another cabinet door flimsy we crawl up to grasp the drawer pull then grabbing the end pull it out swinging it. The contents spraying the counter behind me as I stand over him. It draws up into silence my breath evens and setting the drawer next to his head I look close to his face his lids closed my hanging drawn air.

Careful not to lose sight of his face I crawl over his arm and then back out the kitchen, my feet cold and heavy I pause when I am no longer sure of his eyes being closed. There I wait unsure of gravity, I smile let out my breath his eyes spring open as he sits up on his heels. I hold my breath as he pauses there wiping blood from his lip then licking the rest off before smiling. Still on all fours I now must look up slightly to meet his gaze. He rolls back on his heels and sits on the floor licking his still bloody lip. The world is a sway his body a heat, gravity and rushing forward he pulls me face up out on the floor. Our heads aligned he pulls my body back into the kitchen laying on the floor with me. Along side me rolling his head down my chest coating me with his blood. It's hot scent the fresh taste of my own in my mouth. I was a drowning in lava unable to dry an inch. Unable to be still I twitched in his arms we rocked there the tile scummy wet with my soaked skin. Condensing into our own centers dragging in every inch of existence scrambling for a stable plane three points to find resistance. There was nothing to hold me and the air was heavy in there with his heart and lungs. With what could only be the sucking silence of absence. There was also nothing to hold me there either and rushing back in my hiccup I saw my filthy smile. Nothing washes the truth off. I saw his wet face the fingers over my face cooing to his love the evil of my loins. I am bones snarled with poison veins slugging the cords fouled by a true heart black and rubbery hid in satin night. He caught his breath put his fingers over his mouth proclaimed the only love death could have in flesh was his thirteen and she denied death as well. I lived. It seems regardless but how lucky could one girl be. I thrived in his rage under the weight, down the hallway into the living room turning to beat my fists knees up his ribs. Knocking over the cabinet as I found the wall then sat tipping over the top drawer empty as he flipped the other away still lodged. It hit the couch a clunk we both paused for, I stood and he stood a foot from me our shoulders rising mine up the door his stopping above me. Dropping to his knees he embraced my legs face soft on my thighs. I petted his face slipping down to the floor folding into his lap then pushing him flat. The dingy carpet compacted, stained tearing my knees crouched over him. I'm trying to feel his heart through my thighs. Trying to find his humanity in his face down his neck over the white of his chest. My hands blue waning trembling I hear his wheeze. My thighs throb from the inside resting on what could be marble. I punch him in the face following with my elbow able to remain upright I watch his eyes remain closed. I listen to a wasteland between my feet stepping over him. The cabinet is turned away and turning to watch his body I tug on the drawer handle looking down it's empty but I hear the click and look up to see him point the muzzle towards me as he begins to get up. I rush him, closing my eyes feeling him hit the door with his backside the gun clipping my shoulder before I ram it into his ribs. He begins to cough as I turn to jam my elbow into his head finding the gun a few feet from his right foot. I can't get my hands around his neck and using his mass he pins me laying me face down to take long strokes across my ass. One foot on my back both my wrists gathered up I relax listening to him catch his breath. The gun still about two feet away. Not the crickets nor the birds accompany his hard breaths I lay on the carpet, thinning out in the path to the kitchen. In the strange dusk the dust is prearranged and no rays of light strike the floor for them to dance in. My own lung doesn't stir but my heart ripples out vibrating his foot cold pressing into my lower back. I turn my head look up at him as strikes my face.

The silence is eerie I know I haven't been anywhere the carpet decaying chunky on my cheek. He rolls me over face up and drags me down the hallway I watch the light change the inches of wall grey. The bathroom is open but he wraps his hand around my throat as he steps in then closes the door on our way to the last open door. I fight kicking his free hand before he on top of me retrieving the syringe pinches my slimy hip. I find the fluid but can't stop the rubbery pull. Can't avoid it's detour,

174

faced with melted white it's the cooing raising up the little hairs down my arms I strike at him let my hand fall open surrendering in the carpet. It's not silence but absence. I weight dripping through the floor puddle hissing spitting across the planks. I open my eyes but I am still in his arms, still a muted world devoid of color. Even his eyes, flat, watching me as he lays down beside me on the bed stroking my head his lips turned up in a self satisfied grin as he ate the little blue bird of happiness. Stifled it's singing to please his appetite, to appease the gritty sand of his thoughts. I feel myself smile watch his eyes cool to blue his hand traces my face before closing his eyes. I wait to see his chest rise and fall, counting ,I feel light. I am not bound, slipping off the bed I lay on the wood seeing the box of bullets under the bed. I reach out my hand, I can brush the edges. Turning I use my feet pushing myself sideways. I easily toe it to the closer side and drawing it under my chest I crouch down to peer onto the bed. I stand turning to walk down the hallway I stop in the living room listening paused. The gun is nowhere in sight the drawers still spread the kitchen a mine field of utensils. It's his face around the corner of the hallway I freeze the box in my hand. He smiles, the gun in his hands, he throws it in the living room watches me. I toss the box out across the living room the bullets spraying out little thuds.

He wipes his mouth the little drip red across the back of his hand. I gulp as he closes the distance between us slapping my face. Then backhanding me I step back shielding my face he tells me he knows I want to kill him. He pushes me down on the carpet I can feel two bullets under my back. His hand over my mouth turning me to face the gun he sticks two of his fingers inside me leaning down to tell me how wet I am. He pumps me with his fingers a few times before deciding to spread me over the floor and although his hand is over mine the gun is two inches away. Bracing himself on my shoulder blades he leans in to try to get his limp cock inside me but none of his tugging helps he licks my ear his heavy breath hot raspy I can't understand him but he collapses on my back. I hold my breath feel his ribs expanding let my air out with his. We took 2 more breaths my fingers brushed the gun, his weight shifted thrusting me several inches and I grasped the gun pulling it into my body as he kneeled over me. His hands on the floor along my body he stood up kicking my armpit I curled around his leg the gun under me. Turning over by grabbing his legs, he tried to shake me off, he kicked the couch, and I flew further into the living room. Kneeling I got my hands around the gun flinging open the barrel turning to see him with the other gun loading it with one bullet.   Slamming it, aiming it at me I close my left eye looking down the barrel and finish loading the gun in my hand. I saw him close his right eye before he pulled the trigger. I didn't hear it. It stung, my eye wept but I stood up I stepped forward until the nuzzle rested between his eyes. Not a word I let my lips curl up he was smiling both eyes open. I squeezed the trigger watching his face frozen, lips parted the blood spray out and dot his nose. A heavy smudge, I dropped the gun turning around opened the front door.